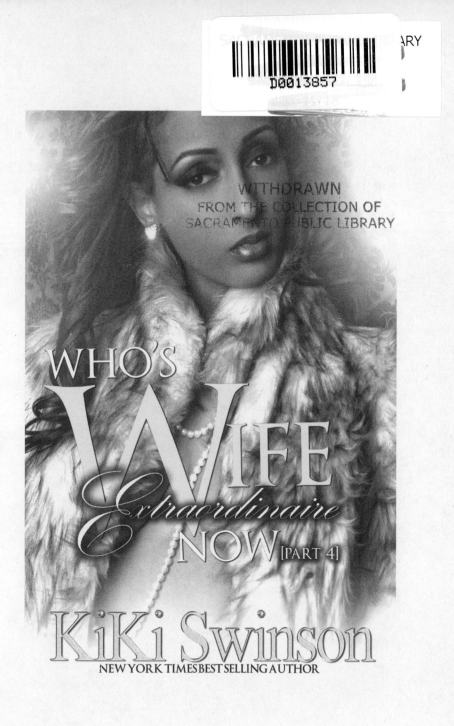

WHO'S WIFE

Extraordinaire

NOW [PART 4]

KiKi Swinson

NEW YORK TIMES BEST SELLING AUTHOR

Publisher's address:

K.S. Publications
P.O. Box 68878
Virginia Beach, VA 23471

Website: www.kikiswinson.net
Email: KS.publications@yahoo.com

ISBN-13: 978-0985349554
ISBN-10: 0985349557

First Edition: October 2017

10 9 8 7 6 5 4 3 2 1

Editors: Letitia Carrington
Interior & Cover Design: Davida Baldwin (OddBalldsgn.com)
Cover Photo: Davida Baldwin

Printed in the United States of America

Don't Miss Out On These Other Titles:

WWW.KIKISWINSON.NET

What Am I Gonna Do Now?

Thirty minutes into my drive to Maryland I kept playing back the events that played out at my house. I couldn't stop thinking about Charlene. Hearing her cry suddenly made me feel sad for her. Were they really going to gang rape her and then kill her after the fact? I can't believe that I was having conflicting feelings for her. I knew she was a sheisty ass bitch, but no woman should ever be subjected to brutal torture and ganged raped and especially while her son was there. I hope this incident doesn't have long term effects on him. Not having his father and mother around to see him grow up is going to be rough for him. Speaking of which, I need to figure out what to do with him. I figured if I took him to the cops, the cops would have a ton of questions for me. And I wasn't in the right frame of mind to be interrogated. Allowing them to interrogate me meant that I was going to be asked, if I knew his parents' names? Where did he live? Where did I pick him up from? How long had I had him in my possession? How old was he? Among other things. The questions were going to be too much for me to handle so going to the nearest police station was off the table.

I turned around in the back seat and looked at Little Leon as he sat there with puffy, watery eyes. Staring at him in his state tugged at my heartstrings. I could tell by just looking at him that he was heartbroken and confused. He wasn't crying as hard as he was when I put him in my car, but he was sniffling a lot. I swear, my heart ached for this kid. He was so freaking precious. So, for the life of me I can't figure out why Charlene would put herself in that predicament and jeopardize the safety of herself and her son. What a fucking idiot she is! Ugh!

"You hungry?" I asked him.

He shook his head, making me aware that he didn't want anything to eat. "Want something to drink?" I pressed him. Once again, he shook his head no, so I turned back around in my seat and looked at the highway in front of me.

"Come on Trice, you gotta figure this thing out." I mumbled to myself. Then it popped in my head. "What's your grandparent's name? Your mommy's mother?" I asked him after I turned around to look at him. He hunched his shoulders, so I turned my head back around to face the traffic. "Ugh! What the hell am I going to do with you?" I said, while gritting my teeth. And then a sick feeling came over me. It felt like I had large knots turning in my stomach. I knew it was anxiety because it engulfed me after I started thinking about the fact that his father Leon had just been murdered and how his mother was being tortured at this very moment. And now I'm left holding the bag. Why me? Why couldn't they just leave me out of all this unnecessary bullshit? It's bad enough that I lost my baby and my sister not even a week ago, so taking on this baggage would be more than I could handle.

"I want my mommy." Lil Leon whined. I looked at him through the rearview mirror because of a sudden traffic jam I had just driven upon.

"Okay baby, don't cry. It's gonna be alright." I said, hoping that my words would calm him down. But it didn't. "I want my mommy now." He began to sob all over again.

Between him crying and me being bumper to bumper in this traffic, I was about to unravel. "Fuck! Fuck! Fuck!" I huffed as I hit the steering wheel. "Why the fuck is there traffic on the highway this time of the night? Everybody is supposed to be at home. Shit!" I continued, shaking my head with mere frustration on my face. I saw a female driver look at me strangely as she sat in the car next to mine. But I could care less. I had bigger issues. One being, I had to figure out what I was going to do with this little boy.

"Does those bad guys still have my mommy?" He continued to sob.

Hearing him ask me if the bad guys still had his mother sent a sharp pain straight to my heart. I was shocked that he was able to comprehend what had transpired back at my house. Knowing this, I knew I couldn't take him back to Maryland with me. My mother would lose her mind if she got this little boy to talk and he told her what went on back at my place. Speaking of my place, I can't imagine how it looked right now. I remember one of the guys saying that he was going to light it up in flames. I had mixed feelings about allowing them to do it. But when I thought about the fact that I could run into problems selling my home once it's revealed that my sister had been murdered there, I figured they'd be doing me a favor by burning it down. My only problem now was finding somewhere to take Little Leon.

"I want my mommy." He said once again. And when I was about to lie to him about taking him back to Charlene, it suddenly dawned on me that I could drop him off at Leon's mother's house. When Leon and I tried to make it officially that he and I were going to be with one another, he took me by his mother's house so I could meet her. Mrs. Bunch was her name. She was a nice, older woman. She lived alone in a two-story house in a middle-class neighborhood. Her house was a good ten-minute drive from this traffic jam I just got myself into.

"Hey sweetie! What about your grandmother? Wanna go and see her?" I said, feeling relieved that I found the solution to my problem.

Little Leon didn't respond to my question but it didn't matter at this point. I was dropping him off to his father's mother's house and that's gonna be the end of that.

After sitting in the traffic jam for close to 20 minutes, I was finally let off the next exit.

Leon's mother lived in Norfolk, near the McArthur Mall so it wouldn't take me long to get there. I wished I had her phone number. But unfortunately, I didn't. At this point, it wouldn't matter either way. I was going to drop this kid off to her and then I'm gonna head back up north to my hometown in Maryland. Good riddance Virginia.

The Drop Off

When I looked at the time on the dashboard of my car, I realized that I had gotten there quicker than I thought. So, while I was pulling my car up alongside the curb, I noticed that all the lights inside of Leon's mom's house were off. But the car she drove was parked in the driveway so I knew she had to be inside.

I sat there for a moment trying to figure out what I was going to say to this lady after she finds out that I am dropping her grandson off to her. I know she's going to have a lot of questions for me, so I needed to be on point when I answered her.

While I was formulating my plan, Little Leon looked out of the backdoor window and noticed that we were parked in front of his grandmother's house and didn't hesitate to let me know that he wanted out of my car asap. "I want my grandma." He yelled while he unbuckled his seatbelt.

7

"Hey, wait, what are you doing?" I tried to utter my words as quickly as possible. But the little boy ignored me. In a matter of 10 seconds, this kid unbuckled his seatbelt, opened the back door and hopped out of it. I swear, I couldn't believe my eyes.

"What the fuck!" I panicked as unbuckled my seatbelt and hopped out of the driver seat. By the time my feet touched the grass Little Leon had already made it to the front door and started ringing the doorbell. "Grandma, open the door. It's me Lil Leon." He yelled from the front porch. Not even a minute later, the upstairs bedroom light was turned on. Seeing this took my anxiety to another level. And when I saw the front room light illuminate, I knew that I was about to come face to face with Leon's mother. The thought of it made me feel uneasy because what was I going to say to her? First of all, I haven't talked to her since she buried Leon. And then on top of that, that I'm dropping her grandson off because his mother is being raped and murdered at my house. Fuck no! I can't say that. I can't open my mouth and tell her that. Shit! That lady would call the freaking cops and then I'm gonna have some explaining to do to them. No way! Not tonight. Not ever. "Fuck this shit! I'm out of here." I mumbled to myself and made a sharp U-turn and ran back to my car. I realized that it would be better for me not to let Leon's mother see me at all. This way I wouldn't have to answer any of her questions. Smart move on my part.

My heart raced at the speed of lighting while I scrambled back into my car. By the time I closed the driver side door, Leon's mother was slowly opening the front door. I watched Little Leon as he faced the front door, waiting for her to open it. Standing between them was a black, metal storm door, so she would have to also open that door to let him into her home. "Come on Trice, get the hell out of here." I instructed myself. Fortunately for me, I left my car running when I hopped out of the car so by the time Leon's mother unlocked the storm door and pushed it open, I had already sped off. I wasn't worried about her recognizing my car because it was dark outside. In her mind, I could've been anyone. And that was the way I wanted it.

It seemed like the further I got away from Leon's mother house, the better I felt on the inside. I mean, it felt like a load was lifted from my shoulders. Leon's kid is with his next of kin and now I'm on my way up north so I can start a new chapter in my life with my family.

Speaking of which, I know my mother and my sister are going to want to know why I came back to Maryland so soon? So, I'm going to tell them I couldn't stand to be in my house all alone. I'm sure they'll believe me. They'll believe anything I say right now because they want me to be with them and I'm fine with it.

Lucky for me, the traffic jam dispersed when I got back on the highway. I figured if I drove straight up Highway 95- North, I could arrive back at my mother's house before one a.m. That is if there's no freaking traffic near Manassas. I guess I will find out.

One hour into my drive, I started thinking about my estranged husband Troy and how we had a perfect marriage before he signed us up for that dumb ass Swap Wives reality show. Look at all of us now. Troy is locked up, Leon is dead and by now Charlene should be dead too. Now tell me how did that happen? Why am I the only one left? And why am I so fucking heartbroken? I didn't ask for none of this shit. I was fine being a wife to Troy because back then, I knew without a doubt that he really loved me. The little things he used to do for me were so beautiful. We didn't really need that money. All we needed was each other. That was it. Now all of that has gone out of the window.

One and a Half Hours Later

I thought I was going to be able to drive back to Maryland without stopping at a rest area or a gas station, but my eyes wouldn't let me. I was so tired that I had to stop at a McDonald's restaurant while I was driving through Fredericksburg, Virginia. Unfortunately for me, the lobby of the restaurant was closed. My only contact with the workers inside was a trip through the drive thru. And ordering something to eat wasn't what I came here to do. Maybe get a cup of coffee, but not a full fledge meal.

It didn't take me long to go through the drive thru to order and pay for my cup of coffee. It also didn't take me long to find a parking space while I prepped my coffee for the road. I had to have the right amount of sugar and cream to give my coffee the right taste.

While I was sitting there, stirring the creamer inside my cup of coffee, I noticed a

12

state trooper had pulled his patrol car up beside my car. He was a middle age white guy and he looked very friendly. I watched him through my peripheral vision as he parked his patrol car and got out of it. For a moment, I thought he was going to head into the McDonald's restaurant, but when he walked around the back of his car and began to walk towards me my heart rate started beating rapidly. "Why the fuck is he walking towards me?" I mumbled to myself while I continued to stare my coffee.

I pretended not to see him and waited for him to get my attention. I figured this way, I won't seem so anxious and paranoid. A few seconds later the state trooper knocked on my driver side window. I pretended I like I was shocked to see him and said, "Oh my God, you scared me!" I spoke loudly through the window.

"Can you roll your window down please?" He asked me.

"Oh, sure." I replied while I powered my window down with one hand and held my cup of coffee with the other.

"What's your name?" He didn't hesitate to ask.

"Trice… Trice Davis." I answered, trying not to sound nervous.

"Can I see your driver's license?" He said.

"Is there something wrong officer?" I asked him while I placed my cup of coffee down into the cup holder between the driver and passenger side seat. A few seconds later, I started digging around in my purse for my wallet because that was where my driver's license was. After sifting through my purse, I found my wallet so I grabbed it and proceeded to pull my license from it. Once I had it in hand I handed it to the officer and waited for him to tell me why he was fucking with me. I mean, it's not like he pulled my car over for speeding. I honestly hadn't done shit wrong.

I watched him as he pointed his flashlight at my ID while he looked it over. Less than a few heartbeats later, he flashed his flashlight at my face. "I see you're from the Virginia Beach area." He commented.

"Yes, sir I am." I replied.

"Did you know that your bottom left taillight is out?"

"No, I'm sorry I didn't know that." I told him and immediately opened my car door. The state trooper stepped backwards a few feet as I pushed my door open. "Are you sure?" I said, making small talk while I closed the car door and walked to the back of my car.

"Yes, I am sure." The state trooper assured me as he followed behind me.

After I saw which light had blown out, I wondered to myself when did the light go out. And while I was trying to jog my memory, my cell phone started ringing while it was in my front pocket, so naturally I retrieved it from my pocket and zoomed in at the caller ID. When I realized it was Detective Grantham, the same guy who was investigating my sister's murder, a dark cloud came over me and it felt like I was about to piss in my pants. I also wondered why he would be calling me this time of the night. I mean, it's not like we had a personal connection where I gave him permission to call me at this hour. Not only that, doesn't he know that I could be asleep? Whatever it was, I wasn't going to find out until a later day.

"Wanna answer that?" The state trooper asked me.

"No, it's fine. It's only my husband trying to figure out where I am." I lied while I shove my cell phone back into my pants pocket.

"Are you sure you want to do that?" He questioned me. "There's a lot of weirdos roaming around here and I would hate to find out that something happened to you on my watch." He pressed the issue.

"Don't worry. As soon as I get back into my car I'm heading home."

"Well, you make sure you do that. And get your husband to change that taillight too. I have a couple of colleagues that aren't as nice as I am. Believe me they will write you a ticket as soon as you can blink your eyes." He warned me.

I chuckled, giving him the impression that I appreciated his humor and his kindness for not giving me a ticket. "Thank you so much officer, I really appreciate you for your kind gesture." I said.

"No problem. Now get home safely." He instructed me, while he handed me my driver's license back.

"I will." I assured him while I held my license in one hand and used my other hand to open the car door. After I got back in my car, I sat there and watched the state trooper crawl back into his car. I sat there for a moment, hoping that he was going to leave before me, but after waiting for a little over two minutes I saw that he had no intentions on leaving any time soon, so I put my car in reverse and then I drove out of there.

I found the nearest exit to Highway 295-north and I took it. Being in that cop's face nearly caused me to have a fucking heart attack. For a moment there, I thought he was going to arrest me. The way he looked at me gave me this eerie feeling. He made me feel like he knew who I was and the incident I allowed to happen back at my home. Thank God, he didn't or else I'd be in the back of his patrol car, instead of my own.

While I think about it, I'm curious to know why he sat there in the parking lot while I drove away? Was he running my license plates to see if my car was stolen? I hoped I didn't spark any suspicion with him after I refused to answer my cell phone after he started ringing. I was a pretty good liar so maybe he did believe me and I'm reading too much into this situation.

As I drove further and further away from that state trooper, the less anxiety I felt. It felt like a mountain of snow had melted away from my shoulders. What a relief!

Fifteen minutes into the drive, my cell phone started ringing again. When I looked back at the caller ID I noticed it was Detective Grantham calling me once again. One part of me wanted to answer it. But then the other part of me refused. After the forth ring I decided to let the call go to voicemail. I figured whatever he

17

wanted with me, he'd let me know in his voicemail message.

What do you know, ten seconds later, the voicemail bell on my cell phone chimed, indicating that he left me a voicemail message. So, I logged into my voicemail box and waited to hear what he had to say. My heart began to beat out of control right after I heard Detective Grantham utter his first word. "Mrs. Davis, this is Detective Grantham. I'm truly sorry for calling you this time of the night, but I'm standing outside of your home and it's engulfed in flames. I don't see your vehicle parked outside the residence so I hope you're not inside. It would be devastating if you are. If you're not here, please call me back. I can be reached at 757-490-5555."

As soon as his voicemail message ended, I backed out of the voicemail function and dropped my cell phone into my handbag that was placed on the passenger side seat of my car.

I swear that after I heard the detective's voicemail message, I wanted to shit bricks. My insides felt like I was about to have a panic attack too. My only question was, why the hell am I getting a call about my house so soon? I expected that one of the fire chiefs would find a way to call me. So, to get a call from Detective

Grantham caught me off God. Whether he knew it or not I wasn't going to call him back. Well at least not right now. It's almost 1 o'clock in the morning and I am exhausted. I'm so tired mentally and physically that when I get back to my mother's house I'm gonna crawl on her living room sofa and close my eyes tight and hope that when I wake back up, everything that I am experiencing now will all just be a nightmare.

I finally reached my mother's house at 1:30 in the morning. Luckily for me, I had a spare key to her front door. Having this key allowed me to walk into her house without her knowing. Thankfully, she didn't turn on her alarm system because if she had, then I'd blow my cover for sure.

Once I was inside the house, I placed my bags on the living room floor, I took my shoes off and then I lied down on the sofa. I heard a lot of movement coming from my mother's bedroom. At one point, I thought she was going to come into the living room. But she didn't and I was glad of that. While I lied there, I tried to block out everything that happened up to this very moment, but my mind wouldn't let me.

Images of the guys that were in my house and the things that they said to Charlene and I made me traumatized. So how was I going to live with myself? How was I going to move forward into my life knowing I gave those guys the green light to kill her in my home? I knew it wasn't my fault that she got tied up with those thugs, but I do take some of the blame that I didn't try to help her. But then again, how could I have helped her? Not to mention, she lied to those guys and told them that I had money in my possession that belonged to them. How fucked up was that? She literally brought those niggas to my house so that they could kill me. That girl was the devil. I just hope that before she took her last breath, she asked the Lord for forgiveness so she could make it into heaven. And if she didn't, too bad for her.

Now as far as I'm concerned, I'm going to have to get a really good game plan, because not only do I have to answer to the cops, my family is going to have a lot of questions too.

It's 1AM

"**D**idn't you tell me that your sister wasn't coming back to Maryland for a few weeks?" I heard my mother's voice say. At first, I thought I was dreaming, but when I heard my mother's footsteps trotter back and forth in the kitchen, I knew that I wasn't. I opened my eyes slowly to adjust to the sunlight creeping through the curtains covering the windows in my mother's living room. She saw me moving around on the sofa so she said, "I think she's waking up now. Trice baby, are you up?"

"Yes mom, I'm up," I replied after I turned my body around to face her.

"Karin honey, I'm putting you on speaker," my mother continued as she walked towards me.

"What are you doing at mom's house? I thought you said you wasn't coming back to Maryland until after you tied up all the loose

21

ends dealing with your house and stuff." Karin yelled through the phone.

"I was. But as soon as I got there I knew that I couldn't be there alone so I got back on the road and came back here." I explained, while I continued to lay there.

"Well, don't move. I'll be home in a couple of hours. Gotta run a few errands for my man this morning." She yelled again.

"You stayed over there last night?" I yelled back.

"Yeah, I did. So, let me get off this phone so I can handle my business." Karin told me.

"All right," I replied.

"Don't forget to stop by the pharmacy and pick up my meds." My mother reminded her. After Karin assured her that she wouldn't forget, they both ended the call. By this time, I had sat up straight on the sofa.

"Want a cup of coffee or hot tea?" My mother asked me as she turned around and headed back into the kitchen.

"Yes, I could use a cup of coffee." I told her.

"So what time did you get here?" Her questions continued while I watched her poured me a cup of coffee from the coffee pot.

22

"I got here around 1:30." I replied without even thinking about it.

"You weren't scared to travel back all this way that time of the night?" She asked as she grabbed a spoon from the utensil drawer.

"No, I wasn't scared. I actually didn't think about it after I decided to come back this way."

"How many cubes of sugar do you want?"

"Three will be fine." I said.

While she dropped three cubes of sugar into my cup of coffee, I noticed the steam as it evaporated into the air and instantly thought about the flames and smoke that engulfed my home. I knew it had to be a horrible sight. I'm just glad that I wasn't there to witness it.

"Be careful now. This coffee is really hot." My mother warned me as she handed the cup of coffee to me.

I took the cup from her and took a quick sip of it. After I swallowed the half-ounce of coffee from my cup, I placed it down on the coffee table in front of me. "How is it?" My mother wanted to know after she took a seat on her favorite recliner. She was nursing a cup of coffee too.

"It's good." I told her. But in all honestly, it was okay. I was never a coffee drinker, but I figured with all the shit I had going on in my life, drinking a cup of coffee would help relax me.

"So how long do you plan on being here?" She changed the subject.

"I don't know. I mean, I really hadn't thought about it. I just knew that I didn't want to stay at the house alone so grabbed a few things from my bedroom, hopped back into my car and headed back this way." I explained.

"You know you don't have to lay on the sofa. I've got two guest bedrooms in house, so pick which one you want to sleep in and let that be the end of it." She said and then she changed the subject. "Tell me something," she started off.

"What is it?" I reluctantly said.

"When you were pregnant, were you 100% sure that Troy was the father?"

"Of course, I was." I lied. Quiet as kept, I was completely unaware who was my baby's father. I lied to Troy about him being the father and then I told the same lie to Leon. I figured that after my baby was born, both men would have to take DNA test. Better safe than sorry, I thought. "What made you ask me that?" I asked her.

"Because of all the rumors I heard."

"Tell me who was running their mouths."
I pressed her. Knowing that someone had been
talking about me behind my back wasn't sitting
well with me.

"Your cousin Craig and his silly wife
Nadine."

"See, I knew it was his gossiping butt. He
loves sticking his nose into my business. He
needs to focus more on his wife and less about
me before I blow up her spot and reveal all of
her secrets." I threatened.

"Baby, don't waste your time with those
two. They're so messy it's ridiculous. And
besides, you've got bigger fish to fry."

"Yeah, I know." I agreed with her.

"Have you decided what you're going to
do with all the stuff you have in your house?"
Her question started up again.

"No not really." I replied, hoping that all
of Troy's things were destroyed in a house fire.

"You might want to hire professional
movers to remove your things from the house.
That way you don't have to do it yourself."

"Yeah, I thought about that too." I lied to
her once again just to keep the conversation
going.

"You know you can stay here with me for as long as you want. Having you back in the house would mean so much to me."

"I know mama." I said and took another sip of coffee for my mug.

My mother sat in her recliner and asked me at least a dozen more questions about how I plan to make the transition from my house back to Maryland? When was I going to file for a divorce from Troy? Am I going to be able to sell the house without Troy's approval? I swear, I was started getting annoyed with the constant questions and at one point I was going to ask her to please leave me alone, but I knew how sensitive she was so I left well enough alone.

Fortunately for me, my mother's house phone started ringing. The nearest phone was in the kitchen so she had to get up and go in there to answer it. "Saved by the bell!" I uttered quietly, so she wouldn't hear me.

"Hello," I watched her say to the caller on the other line. I couldn't hear what the other person was saying, but as soon as my mother said, "Of course not, I was just sitting in the living room talking to my daughter Trice that lives in Virginia." I knew she was either talking to one of her neighbors or a friend from church.

"No, I haven't spoken to her since I left for Maryland a week and a half ago." My mother continued and then she fell silent. To prevent from listening to her entire phone conversation, I grabbed the remote control from the coffee table and powered on the TV. After sifting through a ton of channels I finally decided to watch a church sermon on the Christian channel. T.J. Jakes was the name of the pastor and he sure had a lot of to say.

"God will give you strength when you don't think you can go on." He began to say. And when he uttered those words I gave him my undivided attention.

"A lot of people walk around here like they can handle every situation they stumble across. But let me be the first one to say, that they are sadly mistaken. Before I gave my life to Christ, I would put on my cape like I was Superman and walk around here with my chest pumped up like I was gonna do something. But guess what happened? I ended up making my situation worse than what it was in the beginning. See that's what we do in most cases. But that's not what God wants us to do. He wants us to come to him in prayer and tell him everything we got going on and the minute you end that prayer, he doesn't want you to do anything else because he is going to take care of it. Do you understand what I'm saying? Once you lay down your problems and your burdens, there is nothing else required of you to do. So, sit down. Our father is going to handle everything." He continued.

I swear this man was giving me a powerful message. It was so powerful that I got filled up with the emotions and started crying. I felt the burden of my trials pressuring me to let God handle the situation I was in. So, while I continued to watch the sermon my mother made her way back into the living room. "Baby, what's the matter?" She asked me as she approached me.

With puffy red eyes, I wiped them with the back of my hand and said, "I'm just tired Mama. I'm tired of dealing with all this mess that's coming at me all at once." I said as I began to sob. A huge load of pressure began to weigh heavily on my shoulders. My heart became heavy too. I was one ball of mixed emotions.

"Oh baby, I am so sorry you're going through this." My mother said as she sat next to me and embraced me.

"Mama, I just wanna pack up my things and move somewhere far where no one knows me." I continued sobbing.

My mother hugged me tighter. "Trice darling, running away from your problems isn't going to make them go away. You're gonna have to face them head on and deal with them."

"But I'm not strong like you and the other women in the family." I replied, between sniffles.

"That's why you're gonna have to pray about it and give it to God. He will fix all your problems and give you the peace you need while He's working things out for your good." My mother assured me as she massaged my back in a circular motion.

Everything she was saying about God, I knew to be true but the question was, would God come to my rescue and help me? Especially with all the sins I've committed? Not to mention, that I allowed those guys to kill Charlene. In God's eyes, I pulled the trigger too. But let's just say that He did forgive me of my transgressions and pulled me out of this dark place I'm in, how long would it take Him to turn everything around? I've seen people wait months and years for a breakthrough, so would I have to wait that long too?

My mother sat on the sofa with me for the next thirty minutes trying to cheer me up by giving me words of encouragement. With much determination, she finally got me to calm down and stop crying. But before she released me from her embrace, she prayed for me. And immediately after she ended the prayer with *In Jesus' Name.... Amen,* she kissed me on my forehead and said, "You're gonna be alright baby girl."

"I hope so." I responded nonchalantly.

The Unexpected Happened

When my mother stood up from the sofa, I stood up next to her. "I'm gonna go and use the bathroom." I told her. But then, my cellphone started ringing. I let out a long sigh. "Who could this be this time of the morning?" I said aloud as I leaned down towards the floor to get my phone from my purse. When I had the phone in my hands, I looked at the number and saw that it was Troy calling me from jail. Now I normally don't answer his calls, but for some reason, I wanted to hear what he had to say to me today.

"Hello," I said after I sat back down on the sofa. By this time, my mother had walked back into the kitchen.

"You have a pre-paid call from Troy," the recording said. "If you accept this call please press '5' now." The recording finished.

I pressed the number '5' button and immediately there-after I heard Troy's voice. "Hello." He said.

"Hey, how you doing?" I asked nonchalantly. I really wasn't in the mood to hear his voice but being as though I hadn't spoken to him since my family and I buried my sister Anna, I felt like he may have something new to say to me. An apology for ruining my life would start things off nicely. "What do you want Troy?" I was cold.

"I just got off the phone with my Aunt Sabrina and she said that she saw our house on TV and that it has completely burned down to the ground. Now please don't tell me that's true."

Before I answered Troy, I thought about how it would be damaging on my part if I admit to knowing that our house was on fire, especially since the calls at the jail are always being monitored and recorded. So, I played it off and said, "Don't believe everything you hear. I just left home not too long ago."

"Then why would she tell me that?"

"Troy, I can't answer that. Maybe she just wants to be messy."

"Where are you now?"

"That's none of your business." I replied sarcastically.

"Well, can we talk about us?" He asked me like he was walking on egg shells.

"What is there to talk about? You and I are over, Troy." I hissed, I didn't want to upset my mother by yelling at him.

"Trice, please give our marriage another chance baby. I swear to you that I didn't have anything to do with your sister Anna getting killed. And when I go to court for it, you'll find out that I'm not lying to you."

"Is that all you called me for?" I shut him down. I didn't wanna talk about anything that had something to do with he and I reconciling. That deal was off the table.

"Yes, but can you at least think about what I said?" He pressed the issue.

"Bye Troy." I said and then I ended the call. I placed my cellphone down on the coffee table in front of me and then I looked up and saw my mother walking towards me. "He doesn't want you to file for divorce, huh?" She asked me as she stood in front of the table.

"Yeah, he wants me to give him another chance. Plus, he keeps denying that he had something to do with Anna's death. And by doing that, pushes me farther and farther away from him. I mean, how can he ask me to reconcile with him when he murdered my sister? Does he really think I want to be with a man like that? But what makes my heart turn colder towards him is when I think that that bullet Anna took was intended for me. So again, why would he think I want to be with a monster like him?"

"He thinks that you're weak minded." My mother said.

"Well, he can forget that notion because I'm leaving him and that's final." I said and then I stood back up on my feet. "Let me go to the bathroom before I pee on myself." I continued and headed down the hallway.

"Want me to make you some breakfast while I'm in the kitchen?" She asked me.

"No. I really don't have much of an appetite."

"Well, I'm gonna fix a pot of oatmeal just in case your appetite comes back." She insisted.

After I entered into the bathroom it didn't take me long to pee. And while I was walking back out of it, I decided to take a hot shower. My clothes and things were in the bags laid on the floor by the sofa so I grabbed them and headed back.

Ten minutes into my shower time, my mother started knocking on the bathroom door. "Trice," She yelled from the other side of the door.

"Yes mommy," I yelled said.

"You have a call." She yelled once again.

"Who is it?" I yelled back, after a lump formed in my throat, simultaneously while my heart crashed into the pit of my stomach.

"He says his name is Detective Grantham." She replied.

Anxiety began to engulf me as I stood there underneath the warm water dispensing through the shower nozzle. I wanted to yell at my mother and ask her why the hell did she answer my cellphone, but I knew that would not have been the right thing to do, so I bit my tongue and said, "Tell him I'm in the shower and that I'll call him back."

"I told him that already." My mother explained.

"So, what's the problem? Why is he still on the phone?" I continued to yell, even though I already knew the answer.

"Trice, he said your house caught on fire last night so he really needs to talk to you."

Frustrated by my mom's inability to get rid of that cop, I yelled and said "Mom, tell him that I will call him back as soon as I get out of the shower."

"Sir, she says she'll call you back as soon as she gets out of the shower." I heard her say and then she fell silent. Two seconds later she said, "Trice baby, was going on?"

"Mom, I don't know."

"Well, you're gonna have to hurry up and come out of the bathroom so you can call that detective back." She instructed me and then I heard her walk away from the bathroom door.

After finding out that Detective Grantham was able to get my mom to answer my cell phone nearly gave me a fucking heart attack. And I dreaded leaving this bathroom because as soon as I see her she's going to have a ton of questions for me that I'm not sure how I'm going to answer. To make matters worse, she's going to make sure that I call that detective back. "Damn! How in the hell did I get into this shit?" I uttered quietly just in case she was still standing on the other side of the bathroom door.

I tried stalling my shower time for another 15 minutes, but when the water started getting cold I knew my bathroom time had ran out. So, I stepped out the shower grabbed my towel and dried my body off. After my body was completely dried, I slipped on a pair of panties and the bra to match. I got dressed in today's attire too, which happened to be an Addias tracksuit.

I brushed my teeth moments later, and then I brushed my hair back in the same ponytail

I've been wearing for the past two weeks. So, why switch it up now?

"Trice, you need to hurry up and come out here so you can call that detective back." My mother yelled through the door.

"For God's sake mom, I'm coming!" I snapped. She was getting on my nerves now. Frustrating me to the point of influencing me to possibly have a nervous breakdown.

I counted to the number ten while I got up the nerve to exit the bathroom. And as soon as I uttered the number ten, I took a deep breath, exhaled and then I opened the door. Surprisingly, my mother wasn't standing at the door but she was front and center when I walked back in the living room. She was standing in the middle of floor holding my cell phone with one hand and a kitchen towel that she uses to dry clean dishes. "Is there something you're not telling me?" She didn't hesitate to ask me.

"What are you taking about mom? Of course, not." I lied, simultaneously giving her the sincerest expression I could muster up.

"Did you know anything about your house being burned down before the detective call?"

"Of course not, mom. Don't you think that if I would've known I would not have come back here?" I lied to her again. Was she crazy? I couldn't care less how close we were, there are some things that you must keep to yourself. And telling her what really was going on in my life, wasn't in the cards, especially not now.

"He said he called your cellphone around midnight because he thought that you might've been in the house."

"Maybe he did. But, I didn't get it."

"Well, take this phone and call him back." She instructed me as she handed me my cell phone.

I took my cellphone from her and looked at it for a second. I was dreading to make this call back to the cop but I knew my mother wasn't going to let me get away with it. I went into my call log, found his number and then I called it back. He answered my call after the third ring. He said, "Hello," but my mouth wouldn't move. I swear, I was truly at a loss for words. "Hello," he said once again but my mouth wouldn't open to save my life. My mother heard him when he said hello the second time, so she said, "Answer him." She coached me.

"Hello," I finally said.

"Mrs. Davis, is this you?" He asked.

"Yes, its me." I reluctantly answered him.

"I called you around midnight after I was called to your residence because of a fire."

"My mom just told me." I replied nonchalantly.

"I told one of the firemen that you could've possibly been in the house at that time. Thankfully you weren't. But I must inform you that a body was found and it was burned very badly…"

"Oh no!" My mother blurted out as she covered her mouth. I could see the horror in her eyes.

"A body? No, that can't be. When I left home last night, no one was there." I lied, as my heart rate sped up.

"I'm sorry ma'am, but it was."

"Was it a man or a woman?" My mother interjected and the detective must've heard her because he answered her.

"As far as I know, the body was that of a woman."

"Oh my God! That could've been you." My mother yelled out and started sobbing.

"Do you have any idea who that person could've been?" Detective Grantham wanted to know. But I wasn't about to tell him shit. There was no way in hell I was going to tell him anything.

"No. I don't. Are you sure you even got the right house?"

"Your residence is 821 Levi Circle, right?"

"Yes," I replied, but it was barely audible.

"Well, then I've got the right house. So, I'm gonna need you to do a few things for me."

I hesitated for a moment and then I said, "What is it?"

"You're in Maryland at your mother's place, am I correct?"

"Yes,"

"Okay, well, I'm gonna need you to come down to the precinct so I can get a statement from you and hopefully we can figure out what happened at your home. I spoke with the fire chief too. He says he wants to get a statement from you as well."

"So, when is all this supposed to happen?"

"I'm hoping as soon as possible. Think you can get back down here by tomorrow morning?"

"Tell 'em yes." My mother interjected.

I gave her the look of death when she opened her mouth. She had no fucking idea what type of shit I was in. Why don't she just be quiet?!

"So, can I expect to see you tomorrow?" He uttered.

I hesitated once again. I swear, I wanted to tell this asshole that I wasn't coming any fucking where. But, then I thought about how it would look if I did say it. My mother would look at me like I was fucking insane. And the cop would automatically think I was behind the whole house fire and Charlene's dead body. After weighing the pros and the cons of this situation, I finally said, "Yes, I'll come by your office tomorrow."

"Okay. Sounds great. And do me a favor."

"What's that?"

"I'm gonna need you to bring the clothes you had on last night so we can test them for any accelerant."

"Wait, you want me to bring my clothes to you so you can test them for accelerant?" I asked him, trying to get clarity.

"Yes, exactly." He didn't hesitate to answer.

"So, you've already got it in your mind that I started the fire at my house." I responded in a cynical manner. I mean, what the fuck was up with him? I wouldn't ever burn down my own house.

"No, I don't. But it's just a small formality. That's it."

"Trice, just take him the clothes." My mother interjected from the back ground.

"Yeah, whatever. Is that it?" I asked.

"I think we're almost done." He said and then he fell silent. "Oh yeah, when you bring your clothes back, I want you to give them to the fire and arson investigator. He's the one that's going to test them."

"Is that it?" I asked him once again.

"Oh, one last thing, you might wanna call your insurance so you can file a claim." He suggested.

"That's already on my to-do list." I assured him.

"All right, well I guess that's all I need right now. But if you happen to think of anything please don't hesitate to give me a call."

"I won't." I said and then I ended the call.

When Bad Goes to Worst

Right after I hung up with the detective my mother rushed towards me and gave me an embrace like she wasn't going to let me go. A few seconds later, she started sobbing uncontrollably. "I can't lose another child." She cried out as she laid her head down on my shoulders.

"Mom, calm down. You're not going to lose me." I tried consoling her while I hugged her back. But then she lifted her head back up, "What if the people that killed Anna set your house on fire because they thought you were there? What if that evil person was there to kill you, baby?"

"Mom, let's not jump to conclusions. I'm here and I'm safe with you."

"You know I'm not letting you go back to Virginia by yourself." She told me.

"Yes mom, I already know that."

"I'm gonna call your sister and your aunt Carolyn so they can ride down south with us. I think we should try to get your cousin Craig to go with us too. If people see us with a man, they'd think twice about doing something to us." My mother explained.

I pulled away from my mother's embrace after she mentioned my cousin Craig's name. I don't want that negro in my business. "Mom, you know I don't mess with that fool, especially after he came at me the other day."

"Okay, I'll admit that he was out of line the other day but with everything that's going on, we gotta put that mess behind us. We're family! And family must stick together." She reasoned. I heard the hurt and disappointment in her voice.

"Mom, he's not going with us and that's final." I told her, standing my ground and then I walked away from her. I sat down on the sofa and pretended to be looking at the television. She followed and took a seat on the loveseat across from me.

"Is there something you're not telling me?" She asked as she looked directly at me.

"What are you talking about?" I got defensive.

"When the detective asked you when you'd be able to come back down there so he could take a statement from you, why did you hesitate? You gave off the impression that you didn't wanna go."

Realizing that my mom was onto me, got me feeling uneasy. I felt heat gather around my neck like it was about to choke me. It was unbearable to say the least so I instantly became more defensive. "Would you want to go back to a place where your sister was killed?" I roared. "I have nothing but bad memories from that place. Not only did I lose a baby, I lost my husband too." I continued.

"Trice, I understand everything you're saying right now. And I feel nothing but pain for you. But someone set your house on fire and it was probably to get rid of you. Thank God you weren't there, but sadly someone else was. So, we need to get down to the bottom of it and hopefully prevent someone else from getting killed."

"Mom, can we just leave this alone? I swear, you're giving me a migraine." I spat. I knew what she was saying was the right thing to do, but she doesn't know the whole story. The guys that set my house on fire weren't there to kill me. Well at least, that's what I think anyway. Now I do know for sure that if I utter any information to the cops or the fire chief about who was the cause of the fire at my house, those guys will put me on their hit list. And that's what I'm trying to prevent.

"I'll leave it alone for now but as soon as your sister gets here, we're gonna talk about it." My mother warned me and then she stood up from the loveseat. Before she could take a step, the front door opened and my sister Karin appeared. "What's going on here? What are we talking about?" She asked as she entered into the house.

Instead of giving Karin a smile and a warm welcome, I rolled my eyes because I was not in the mood to talk about the conversation I just had with the cop back in Virginia. "Your sister got a call from the homicide detective that's investigating Anna's murder and he didn't call to talk about Anna's killer, he called to inform Trice that someone set her house on fire last night right after she got on the road to drive back here." My mother blurted out.

Karin closed the front door and stood there in shock. She zoomed right in on me. "Are you guys serious right now?" Karin asked.

"That's not it. They found a dead body in her home too. It was burnt to a crisp." My mother continued as she stood a few feet away from Karin.

"Oh my God! This is scary!" Karin said as she covered her mouth with both hands. "I'm so glad you decided to come back here last night. I mean, do you know what it would've done to mom and I, if the cop called and told us that it was you? Girl, we'd be walking around here like zombies."

"The detective wants her to come back to Virginia by tomorrow so he can take a statement from her but she doesn't want to go." My mother continued to reiterate.

"I don't blame her mom. She's been through a lot. Would you wanna go right back to that God forsaken place after all she's been through?" Karin sided with me. Boy, was I glad of that.

"Thank you for that Karin. Mom, doesn't understand how much this whole ordeal has taken out of me. I really would like to take a trip out of this country and never come back." I said.

"Stop talking crazy because that will never happen. Not over my dead body, anyway." My mother told us. She seemed very adamant too.

"So, does the cop know whose body was found in your house?" Karin asked after she took a seat on the sofa next to me.

"No, he doesn't." I replied.

"But he did say that it was a woman's body." My mother interjected.

"So, you don't know who that could've been?" Karin asked me.

"No, I don't." I said, trying to give her the sincerest expression I could muster up. See, Karin knows me like a book. And among other things, she knows when I'm lying to her. So, I knew I had to pay extra attention to my body language while I answered her questions.

"Do you have other friends or neighbors that you talked to while you lived there? Maybe, they stopped by while the person was there and got pulled into the crossfire." Karin theorized and then she looked at me and my mother to get our reaction.

My mother spoke first. "That's a little too farfetched for me."

"Well, I don't believe anyone was there. I think the cop said it to get me back to Virginia so he and the fire chief could determine if I started the fire or not." I said, hoping my reason would throw both my mother and my sister Karin off track. I cannot let them find out that I knew about Charlene's body being in my house. At this point, I am forced not to trust anyone but myself.

"I don't think that detective would make up a story like that just to get you back in Virginia. He's a state employee. An officer of the courts. Trust me, if he said that a woman's body was found in the house, then I believe him." My mother concluded.

Karin ignored what our mother said and asked me when was I leaving to go back to Virginia?

"I guess, I'm gonna head out of here tomorrow morning."

"You know I'm going with you, right?" Karin insisted.

"We're all going." My mother's voice boomed.

"Who are you talking about mama?" Karin asked her.

"She wants Craig and Aunt Carolyn to ride with us." I spoke first.

"That's right. We need a man to go down there with us this time around. That woman's body that was found in Trice's house could've been her instead."

"But it wasn't Ma," I interjected.

"Ma, if Trice doesn't want Craig to ride with us then let it go."

"What if something happens?"

"Mom, I don't care what you say because Craig isn't going and that's final." I stepped in.

Before my mother could open her mouth to utter another word, Karin held her pointer finger in the air and said, "Ma, just leave it alone please."

"You girls will listen to me one day." She warned us and then she stormed out of the living room.

Trust Issues

After my mother walked back into the kitchen, Karin leaned in towards me and said, "Don't be so hard on her. You know she means well."

"I know she does. But sometimes she just goes overboard and with everything I've got going on right now, I can't deal with it." I told Karin.

"That's understandable. But let me ask you something…."

"What is it?"

"Did you have something to do with that fire?" Karin asked me while she starred directly into my eyes.

I swear, I almost shit in my pants. But at the same time, I wasn't going to tell her what really happened. I knew how my sister Karin operated. She'd keep the information I'd give her confidential until my mother backs her into a corner. So, I'll kept my secret close to my heart and deny any involvement with that fire.

I know she doesn't believe me because of how she looked at me. But I wasn't fazed by that. I had to stand my ground and that's what I did.

"Did the detective really say that they found a woman's body in your house?" She wouldn't let up. She wanted more information then what I was trying to give her.

"That's what he said." I replied nonchalantly, trying not to break a sweat.

"And you don't find that odd?" Karin pressed the issue.

"Yeah, I do. But what else do you want me to say?"

"Does the detective have any idea who it was?"

"No. He said that her body was chard beyond recognition."

Karin let out a long sigh. "Damn! That's scary!"

"Yeah, I know." I reacted, trying to appear gracious like I had just dodged a bullet.

Before Karin could utter another word, our mother entered back into the living room area where we were. "It sure is and that's why I'm gonna ask Craig to drive back down to Virginia Beach with us." She said adamantly.

"Mom! Craig is not going with us and that's final!" I yelled at her, as if I was spitting hot venom out of my mouth. This was my breaking point with her.

"Don't you dare talk to me like that!" My mother shot back.

"Mom, I apologize for yelling, but you're stressing me out." I told her.

"Ma, just leave it alone. If she doesn't want Craig to go, then respect her wishes." Karin added.

"You two are stubborn just like your father was." My mother said and then she stormed back into the kitchen.

Karin waved our mother off with her hand as soon she turned her back on us and walked away. I had to give it to her, she was one tough cookie. As long as I could remember, she has always stood up to anyone that stood in her way. When my father was alive, she ran our household with an iron fist. Telling Karin and I that we were stubborn like our father was a joke. Hands down, she was the one who was stubborn.

"I don't think we should take mom with us when we get back on the road." Karin said.

"I was thinking the same thing. But how are we going to leave without her knowing?" I questioned Karin.

"We can sneak out of here before she gets up in the morning." She replied and then she thought to herself for a moment. "Wait, that's not going to work. You know she gets up between 6 o'clock and 6:30 in the morning? So, our best bet would be to leave later on tonight." She continued.

I went into thought mode after Karin laid the cards out on the table. Leaving later tonight doesn't sit well with me. I don't wanna be driving back down to Virginia Beach at night. It's bad enough that I have to go back there. So, to leave when it is pitch black outside isn't how I want to face my situation back in that city. For one, it's gonna be creepy and two, traveling at night puts me at a disadvantage when I want to keep an eye out for anyone trying to bring harm to me. "I think it's better if we leave tomorrow morning." I told her.

"Trice, if we leave in the morning, Mom isn't gonna take us out of her sight." Karin pointed out.

"We can tell her that we're gonna go to the store and that we'll be right back. From there we'll hop on the road and head back down south."

"I don't think that's gonna work."

"It will. Don't worry." I assured her.

My mother finally finished cooking the oatmeal and served Karin and I both a bowl of it. She even took it a step further and brought the bowls of oatmeal to us. She handed me the first bowl and then she handed the second bowl to Karin. "Mom, this looks really good." Karin told her.

"Yeah, it sure does," I agreed even though I didn't have an appetite for it.

"You girls be careful because it's extremely hot." She warned us and then she turned around and walked back into the kitchen.

"Mom, why don't you sit down and have a bowl of oatmeal with us?" Karin said.

"I've gotta clean up this kitchen. You know I don't like leaving my kitchen dirty."

"Mom, there's nothing to clean." Karin said while she looked at our mother as she rearranged things around the kitchen. "She's so O.C.D." Karin continued after she turned around and faced me.

I chuckled a little to make it look like I was entertained by what she had just said. But in reality, I was mentally somewhere else. I couldn't take my mind off everything that was unfolding back in Virginia Beach. Not only was I supposed to sit down and talk with the cop, I was told that I had to speak with an arson investigator too. The thought of sitting in a room with those people made me sick on the stomach. Why won't they just leave me alone? I haven't done anything to anyone. So why am I always being harassed? I know one thing though, the fact that I have to go and see these people only means one thing, and that is, I have to have my story intact. I can't go there and let them dominate me in the interview. When I walk in the room with them I'm gonna have to act like I'm fearless. And I'm gonna have to act like I'm in control. Because if I show the slightest bit of intimidation, I know they will eat me for lunch.

"What's on your mind?" Karin interrupted my thoughts.

"I was just thinking about that long ride back to Virginia." I lied. And then I put a spoonful of oatmeal into my mouth.

"If you don't feel like driving, you know I'll do it for you." Karin insisted, while she spoke in a whisper like tone.

"I think I might take you up on that offer." I whispered back after I swallowed the mouthful of oatmeal.

Karin smiled as she picked up the remote from the coffee table. "Let's find something fun to watch." She said and then she started sifting through the channels.

"Yeah let's do that." I replied and hoping at the same time that whatever TV show we started watching, that it takes my mind off everything that's weighing on my heart. I swear I cannot wait until all of this is over so I can move on with my life. Damn! I can't wait for the day to come.

The Drive Back to VA.

The following morning, I opened my eyes around 6 am because I couldn't get a decent amount of sleep. I literally tossed and turned all night thinking about what I had to do after I crossed the Virginia's state line. Since I was sleeping on the sofa, which was near the front door, I figured I could slip out the door without Karin or my mother hearing me leave. But leaving this house without Karin wouldn't go over well with her so I got up and walked quietly to the bedroom where she was asleep. Thankfully the bedroom door wasn't locked, so after I turned the knob and pushed the door open I tiptoed over to the

58

bed and shook her gently. "Come on, let's go." I whispered to her.

She lifted her head slowly and wiped both of her eyes with the back of her left hand. "What time is it?" She whispered back as she blinked both of her eyes.

"It's a little after 6 o'clock. So, come on before mom wakes up." I told her.

"A'ight," she said and then she eased out of the bed quietly. "Where are you going?" She whispered while I was heading out of the bedroom.

"To the bathroom. I gotta pee and then I'm gonna wash my face and brush my teeth." I told her, my voice barely audible.

"Don't be too loud. You know mama sleeps light." Karin warned me.

"I know what I'm doing." I told her and then I left.

Immediately after I walked out of the room and closed the bedroom door, I tiptoed to the hallway bathroom. It didn't take me long to pee, wash my face and brush my teeth, so I was out of there in a matter of three minutes. Thank God, I took a shower the night before, because if I hadn't, my mother would've wondered why I was taking a shower so early. Bathing early in the morning, could only mean two things. The first thing is, you gotta get dressed because you got to go to work or you got somewhere important to be. And since I didn't have a job, I had somewhere important to be; heading back to Virginia.

Now that I took care of my business in the bathroom, I went back into the living room, I folded my blanket and placed it and my pillow back inside the hallway closet. Right after I closed the closet door, I saw movement through my peripheral vision. My heart dropped into the pit of my stomach and when I turned around to get a better look, I saw Karin as she headed towards me. I took a deep breath, as I placed my right hand on my chest and then I exhaled. "Girl you scared me to death." I told her.

She smiled and tapped me on my shoulder. "Stop being so scary." She chuckled.

"I can't help it." I whispered as I walked back towards the sofa because that's where I left my purse.

"Girl, just come on here." Karin instructed me as she tugged on the back of my shirt.

"I'm coming." I continued to whisper as I grabbed my things. Once I had my purse, the plastic bag containing my clothes from the night before and my car keys in hand, I tiptoed behind Karin as she headed towards the front door.

When I got within arms-reach of the Karin she opened the door quietly and tugged on my shirt as she made her way onto the front porch. Since I was the last one leaving out of the house I was left with the task of closing the front door behind us, so I closed it as softly as I could. "Hurry up before mom gets up." Karin instructed me.

"I'm trying," I told her and then I pulled the front door shut.

Immediately after I closed it, I raced off the front porch behind Karin. "Whose car are we taking?" She asked me.

"Let's take yours." I insisted. I wasn't in the mood to drive. And besides that, I wanted to fly under the radar when I arrived back in Virginia Beach. No one knows how my sister's car looks, so this is an ideal situation to be in especially if there's a target on my back.

"A'right, let's go." She replied and then we hopped into her vehicle.

"Mom, is gonna be fucking pissed once she gets up and realizes that we left her here." Karin pointed out as she started up the ignition and drove away from the house.

"Yeah, I know. So, I'm not answering my phone when she calls." I said.

"I'm not either." Karin continued as she made a right turn onto the next street over. Three and a half miles later, Karin and I were on highway 495-South, heading back down south to Virginia. I sat there in the passenger seat and wondered how everything was going to play out once I got back to Virginia Beach. I even thought about how my home was going to look once I got a chance to see it. Was it gonna be half burnt? Or a pile of ash? I figured that however it was going to look, it wasn't going to be my house anymore. My ex-husband Troy destroyed the sanctity of our home after he fucked Charlene. I will never forgive him for that. Fucking bastard!

"You alright over there?" Karin asked me.

"I will be after I put all this mess behind me." I told her.

"I don't see how you've put up with it this long."

"I don't either." I said and then I fell silent. "Do you know that if Troy wouldn't have signed us up for that stupid ass reality show, we'd still be married, I'd be pregnant and we'd still be living in that house?"

"Do you think Troy was the father of the baby?"

"I really can't say. Troy didn't want me to get a DNA test because he said he knew he was the father. I believe he didn't want me to take the test because he didn't want to find out that Leon was really the father."

"Would you would've stayed with Leon if he was the father?"

I let out a long sigh. "Yes, I would've. I actually fell in love with him in that little bit of time. He was a good man. And he treated me like a queen every chance he had."

"Do you regret ever getting married to Troy?"

"No, I don't. I loved Troy too. But, I will say that the love I had for Leon was much more intense than the love I felt for Troy."

"Have you heard anything else from Leon's wife Charlene?" Karin asked me. I swear, when she uttered Charlene's name a huge knot formed in my stomach. But I had to remain cool so I did what anyone in my position would do and that was to tell a lie. "Nah, I haven't heard anything from her. It's like she fell off the face of the earth and I'm glad of that." I answered.

"If you wanna know my opinion, that bitch was the mastermind that screwed up both of y'all's marriages. It was like she wanted so desperately to have what you had. She wanted to be you."

"I knew that from day one."

"Well, she can hang it up because she'll never be like you sis. She's a fucking wanna be! A fraud!" Karin ranted on while I knew for a fact that Charlene would never be like me because she was dead. A burnt-up corpse. I just hoped she made things right with God. Because if she hasn't, then she's definitely on her way to hell! Dumb bitch!

Was it Arson or Not?

After two hours into the drive back to Virginia Beach, my mother finally called my cellphone. She allowed it to ring six times before she disconnected the call. A few seconds later, she called Karin's cellphone. Karin looked at her phone and then she looked at me. "Should I answer it?" She asked me.

"No." I protested. "Remember we agreed that we weren't going to do it." I continued.

"Aaaaa' right." She replied after she thought to herself for a moment and then she placed her cellphone back into the cup holder.

"Stay focused." I said and then I turned my attention towards the highway in front of us.

"I am. I am." She tried assuring me. But I knew we were going to have this problem again. Karin didn't have a backbone when it came to our mother. Our mother has always controlled Karin. And it has gotten worse since our other sister was murdered. I believe in my heart of

65

hearts that once I moved back to Maryland our mother is going to do the same thing to me. I guess this is her way of keeping us close to her. And now that I think about it, I'd probably do the same thing if I had children. Too bad, I'm not able to make those judgement calls now. But I'm certain that God will bless me to get pregnant again.

While my sister and I continued our drive down south our mother called our cellphones at least another ten times each. She even left us a few voicemail messages. In one of her messages she threatened not to speak to Karin and I for a month if we didn't call her back. I'm sure that she knew by now that Karin and I had gone back to Virginia without her so I'm sure she's livid. But whether she knew it or not, leaving her back in Maryland was a very wise thing to do because she wouldn't be able to handle all the shit that's going on back in Virginia. Motherfuckers are getting killed just for breathing too much. And I can't put my mother in that kind of predicament. I wouldn't be able to live with myself if something were to happen to her. So, what's done is done.

We finally arrived in Virginia Beach around 10 am. Curious as to how badly my house was burned, I told Karin to take me by there. My heart rate picked up speed as soon as Karin drove onto my street. My home was the fifth house on the left so as we drove closer to it I was beginning to feel nauseous. I close my eyes, took a deep breath and then I exhaled. But before I opened my eyes, I heard Karin gasp and then she said, "Oh my God! Your house is destroyed."

After hearing her words, I opened my eyes quickly and when I saw what she saw I honestly couldn't put my thoughts into words. So, Karin did it for me. "Your entire house is burnt up." She started off saying as she pulled her car alongside the curb. Immediately after she parked her car, she crawled out of the driver's seat and stood on the sidewalk so she could get a better look. I crawled out of the car a couple of seconds later and walked over to where she was standing. I swear, this whole scene was too hard to take in. "Trice, your house is completely destroyed." Karin continued as she searched every inch of it with her eyes.

"I know. When the cop called me yesterday, I had no idea that my house would like this." I commented.

"Why do they have yellow tape wrapped around the trees?" She wanted to know.

"Because they don't want anyone going near the house. I guess this is what you call a crime scene."

"Who would do this to you?" Karin's questions continued.

"I would like to know that myself." I said, even though I already knew the answer.

"I can see parts of your living room sofa from here."

"Yeah, I can see it too." I mentioned.

"I wonder where they found the ladies' body? Did they tell you?" Karin asked me.

"No, the detective I spoke with didn't tell me." I answered her.

Seeing the level of damage to my house was far from what I expected. My entire home was nothing but a big pile ash. All I can think about was how much of Charlene's body was left for the firemen to pull out. One part of me was happy because she got what she deserved. But then the soft and passionate side of me felt sorry for what happened to her. I especially feel sorry for her son because he won't be able to have her in his life as he gets older. I can only hope that his grandmother will feel that void for him.

"Karin, come on. Let's get out of here." I said as I grabbed her hand.

"Where are we going now?"

"To the precinct to talk to that cop."

"Alright, well let's go." She said and then we turned around and headed back to her car.

When Karin and I were getting back into her car, a Caucasian man driving a Virginia Beach, fire and rescue SUV drove up. He was coming from the opposite direction so he parked his truck in front of my sister's car. He got out of his vehicle and approached Karin's car. "Hi, my name is John Wells." He said and leaned slightly into the passenger side window and shook my hand and Karin's hand. "I am one of the fire and arson investigators for the city of Virginia Beach. So, by any chance are anyone of you ladies named Trice Davis?" He asked.

"Yes, I'm Trice Davis." I spoke up.

"Okay great. Could I get you to get out of the car and walk back over to my SUV so I can ask you a few questions?" He continued.

"Yes of course," I said and then I stepped back out of Karin's car.

"Let's go over here." He said as he pointed towards his truck.

I followed him to the hood of his SUV and that's where he pulled out a black, handheld recorder and off loaded a slew of questions on me. "Before I began, I want to let you know that this interview will be recorded and any information you give me will be used to further my investigation. Understood?" He said.

"Yes, I understand." I told him, my voice barely audible. I was a nervous wreck. I wasn't prepared to talk to this man so soon. I was supposed to get with him after I left the precinct. But no, this motherfucker comes from out of nowhere with a bunch of questions in hand and a handheld recorder to record my answers. How much more screwed up could my life get right now? I swear, I was ready to tell this guy that I'd have to catch up with him later, but I knew that wouldn't fly over well with him so I stood there and prayed to God that he'd help me with this interview. "Ready?" He asked me.

"I guess, so." I replied and that's when he pressed the record button on the recorder and placed it on the hood of his vehicle. "My name is John Wells and I'm a fire and arson investigator for the south region of Virginia Beach. I'm here with Trice Davis, the home owner of 821 Levi Circle, in Virginia Beach, the zip code for the property is 23455. The time now is 10:24 am," he started off and then he went into question mode. "Mrs. Davis, will you tell me how long have you lived in the house located on 821 Levi Circle, Virginia Beach, Virginia?"

"My husband I bought this property 7-years ago." I answered him and then I looked back at Karin who was sitting in the driver seat of her car watching the investigator and I. She smiled and winked her eye at me as if to say that I was going to be all right and that she had my back. Unbeknownst to her, I was knee deep in shit and if I wasn't careful, I was going to be in over my head before I knew it.

"Where is your husband now?"

"He's in jail."

"How long has he been in jail?"

"A little over a month now, I guess."

"What is he in jail for?"

"Conspiracy to committing murder and a few other charges."

"How is your relationship with him?"

"Let's just say that I'm filing for divorce."

"Does anyone else live at this residence with you?"

"No."

"Can you tell me who was the last person that left your house?"

"I'm sure it was me. No one else has a key to my house." I replied nonchalantly.

"Did you start that fire?"

"No, I didn't."

"Do you have any idea how this fire started?"

I hesitated for a moment and then I said, "No."

The investigator saw my hesitation so he hurled another question at me. "Do you have any enemies?"

I hesitated once again because I didn't know how to answer that question. My first thought was to tell him I did. And then give him the rundown on everything that happened to me, Troy, Leon and Charlene after we did the reality show. But then I decided against it, because I knew Charlene's body was found in my house. And how would I be able to explain that? So, I said, "the only enemy I can think of right now would be my soon-to-be ex-husband."

"So, you're telling me that your estranged husband could've had something to do with burning the house down?"

"He could have." I lied, knowing Troy didn't have shit to do with it. But hearing that excuse coming from the investigator's mouth sounded plausible.

"What makes you say that?"

"Because he put a hit out on my life after he was arrested for shooting a longtime friend of his and my sister Anna."

"Will you explain?"

"While my husband was in jail he paid a person to come to my house to kill me, but the person shot and killed my sister Anna after she opened the front door because he thought she was me."

"I'm sorry to hear about your loss."

"I'm okay, but thank you," I said.

"When did this shooting incident occur?"

"About two weeks ago."

"Did you get a look at the perpetrator that shot your sister?"

"No, I didn't."

"Do you feel that because the perpetrator did a botched the job in executing you that he came back and set your house on fire in effort to kill you?"

"I've thought about that."

"Did the homicide detective tell you that my guys found skeletal remains of a woman in one of the bedrooms after they put out the fire?"

"Yes, he did." I replied, this time without hesitating.

"Would you happen to know who that was?"

"No," I said, giving him the sincerest expression I could muster up without hesitating. I needed this investigator to believe everything I had to say. He held the cards to freedom in his hands.

"So, you're telling me that you have no idea who that woman could've been?"

"No, I don't." I replied, sticking to my story. I mean, did this guy really think that I was going to give him a different answer? I may be a young woman, but I wasn't a fool. "Have you guys figured out who she was?" I asked him.

"No, we haven't. But I'm positive that we'll know by the end of the day." The investigator said confidently.

"Well, when you do, please let me know." I insisted like I wanted to solve this mystery as bad as he did.

"But of course," he replied as he looked down at his black, metal clipboard. "I think this is about it," he said as he scanned down the through his list of questions.

"Okay, well if you need anything else please don't hesitated to call me." I insisted

"Awesome, give me your number." He said.

"The area code is 757-555-2031." I told him while I watched him wrote my cellphone number down on the paper he had the questions on. After he finished, he reached into his jacket pocket, pulled out his business card, and then he handed it to me.

"If you have any more information for me, please call me." He instructed me.

"Sure. I can do that." I said and then I took the card from his hands and shoved it down into my front pants pocket.

"All right, well I wanna thank you for your time." He continued and shook my hand.

I gave him a half smile. "No, thank you." I told him.

"Oh wait, I need to the clothes you had on the night the fire started."

"They're in the back seat of my sister's car." I said and then I turned around and started walking back towards Karin's car. The investigator followed me. After I opened the back-passenger side door, I grabbed the white trash bag that contained my clothes and handed it off to him.

"Everything is in here?" He wanted to know.

"Yes, it is."

"Okay, well thanks again. I will call you as soon as I finalize my investigation."

"Sounds good." I said and shook his hand one more time.

While I closed the back door to Karin's car, I watched as the investigator walked back to his truck and placed the plastic bag that contained my clothes inside of the SUV. Immediately after he closed the door of his truck, I hopped back inside of Karin's car and watch him as he walked towards my home. After he ducked down underneath the yellow crime tape, he headed around the side of the house. I knew then that he was heading towards the back of my house. My guest room to be exact. And boy did this move stir up the knots in my stomach. I knew I couldn't sit here and watch him sift through all the debris from that room so I told Karin that I was ready to leave. "As you wish," she said and then she drove away from my house.

More Questions

As Karin drove out of my neighborhood, she started questioning me about the conversation I had with the arson investigator. "How are you feeling right now?" she started off.

"I can't really say." I told her while I looked at the houses that we drove by.

"Did he get you any closer as to how the fire started or give the identity of the lady they found in your house?"

"He said that he won't know the woman's identity until later on today. I suppose that's when the coroner is going to let him know."

"What about your house?"

"He's still trying to figure that out, which is why he had a bunch of questions for me to answer."

"I think Troy had something to do with it."

"The coroner asked me if I thought he did it, so I told him it wouldn't surprise me if he did."

"You know what? If that sack of shit did this to your house I would make sure they give his ass the death penalty." Karin huffed. I could see the resentment in her eyes for Troy. I'm sure she wants him out of my life just as much as I do.

I wanted to comment and agree with what Karin was saying about Troy, but Troy didn't have anything to do with burning down the house. So, I turned my attention back to the houses we passed on the way to the police precinct. Karin continued to bash Troy. I on the other hand, just sat there and listened to her rants. Boy did she have a lot to say about him. "I remember when you first met Troy. You were all happy and shit because he took you on a couple dates at some expensive restaurants and bought you flowers. Not too long after that, he started taking you shopping at all your favorite clothing stores. And then, when he bought you that 2-carat diamond ring and proposed to you at your birthday party in front of all of us, you thought you were on cloud 9. But what did I tell you, after that?"

"I don't remember." I replied nonchalantly because I really didn't want to entertain what she was saying. I had bigger fish to fry. And getting through the interview I was about to have with that homicide cop was it.

"I told you not to be blinded by all the material stuff he's buying you because something about him wasn't right to me. But you didn't believe me because if you had, then we wouldn't be having this conversation right now. You thought I was hating on you. But look at you; you lost your baby, you're minus one sister, you have a house that's completely destroyed and a husband that's in jail for murder. How fucked up is that?"

"Did you really have to go there?" I asked her. I don't have to be reminded about how fucked up my life was. I know what's going on.

"Look sis, I'm sorry for what I just said. I'm just upset that you gotta go through all this unnecessary bullshit. I wish all of this would go away."

"It will. Don't worry." I said calmly hoping she'd follow my lead. But while I was two words into changing the topic of discussion, her cellphone started ringing. She grabbed it from the cup holder and zoomed in on the caller ID. "It's mama, isn't it?" I asked her.

"Yup. It sure is." She replied.

"You wanna answer it, don't you?" I tested her.

"Kinda. I really just want her to know that we're all right." Karin tried to reason with me.

"Fuck it! I don't care what you do. We're here now." I told her.

Before Karin's cellphone rang for the third time she answered it and immediately put the call on speaker so I could hear it. "Hello," she said.

"I am so angry with you and your sister!" Our mother's voice boomed. "Why are you just now answering my phone call? Do you know I've been worried sick about you two?"

"Mom, Trice and I are fine."

"Yes mom, we're fine." I chimed in.

"Why did you girls leave me? And don't you lie to me!" My mother continued with her tongue lashing.

"Mom, we left you at the house because we didn't want you to take on more stress by coming back here and dealing with all this mess that Trice has on her plate." Karin explained.

"Listen child, I don't need you or your sister making decisions for me. I can handle myself. Understand?" She replied sarcastically.

"Mom, trust me we did you a favor." I chimed in once again.

"Trice you hush, before I start on you." She threatened.

"Mom, check it out, Trice just had her interview with the fire investigator, she saw the house and now we're on our way to talk to the detective. And as soon as we're done with that, we're gonna call you back." Karin told her.

"Did you guys take pictures of the house?" My mother wanted to know.

"Yeah, I took some." Karin replied.

"I didn't." I uttered loud enough for only Karin could hear me.

"Send them to my phone so I can get a look at them." My mother insisted.

"Okay, I'll send them as soon as I get off the phone with you." Karin told her.

"Did the investigator say who was in Trice's house?" My mother's questions continued.

"No, he said he's going to have that information for her later on today." Karin advised her.

"Well, you girls be careful. And call me as soon as you leave the police station." My mother instructed.

"Okay. We will." Karin assured her and then they both ended the call.

The drive to the police precinct only took us thirteen minutes. Immediately after she parked her car in one of the visitor's parking spaces, she turned the ignition off and then she looked at me and said, "Are you ready?"

"Not really," I replied truthfully. Shit, let's be honest here, I wasn't trying to go in that building. With all the stuff I know, Detective Grantham could throw me in jail and throw away the keys; and I can't have that. I need to keep my freedom. So, whatever it takes for me to have that, I will do it.

Inside the lobby of the police precinct, I was greeted by a uniformed female officer sitting behind a glass window. "How can I help you?" She said.

With Karin in tow I smiled at the lady and said, "I have an appointment to see Detective Grantham."

"Your name?" The officer asked.

"Trice Davis."

"Have a seat and I will let him know that you're here." She told me.

"Thank you." I replied and then I walked over to a nearby seat and sat down in it.

Karin followed suit. "I hope this doesn't take long." Karin said.

"I was just thinking the same thing." I replied. I was literally dreading this conversation I had to have with this cop. If he starts treating me like a suspect then I'm going to end the interview on the spot.

"Think he's going to put you in one of those rooms with the glass on the wall so other detectives can monitor your interview with him?"

"I have the slightest idea."

"Think they might let me go in the interview room with you?"

"I'll ask."

"If they don't, it's okay. The main thing is that you go in there and help him figure out who burned your house down."

"That's exactly what I'm going to do."

"Trice Davis," the male detective yelled across the lobby.

I stood up on my feet. Karin stood up next to me. And then we both started walking towards Detective Grantham. When we were within arms reach of him, he looked at Karin and said, "Sorry, but she's the only one that's authorized to come beyond this door."

"Oh okay." She replied. I could tell that she was a little disappointed. So, I turned towards her and said, "I won't be long."

"All right," she said and then she turned around and headed back towards the seats we were sitting in behind the detective called my name.

"Follow me please," he said as he led me down the hallway. He escorted me to the last room that sat on the left side of the hallway. After he opened the door, he instructed me to have a seat in a wooden chair and then he told me that he'd be right back.

Following the detective's instruction, I took a seat in the cold ass chair and from there I started thinking about how these motherfuckers got me cornered in this tiny ass room. They literally had me where they wanted me, which makes me wonder what kind of questions they're gonna bombard me with? Whatever they are, I know I'm gonna need to stay on point and I can't let them see me sweat. Because if I do, I know they're gonna bury me. "Trice, remember you can't fall under pressure. So, be ready to play their game or else." I mumbled to myself, making sure I couldn't be heard. Interrogation rooms always came equipped with cameras and recording devices throughout the room.

While I searched the room with my eyes, Detective Grantham strolled back in the room with a clipboard in his hands. He smiled and said, "I'm back."

I gave a half smile because I wasn't feeling him with that smile he was giving me. I know what his intentions are concerning this interview, so he needs to cut to the chase. "Are you about to start the interview?" I asked him.

"Yes, I am." He replied as he took a seat in the chair opposite of the table that was between us.

"So, what do you need to know?" I didn't hesitate to ask. I felt like I had to paint the picture that I wasn't here to waste his time nor had I had anything to hide from him. But in reality, I was scared shitless. I knew that if I stumbled on one of his questions, I might blow my whole cover. Not only would I have to deal with catching criminal charges, I would also be on Kevin's kill list. Before I left out of my house, he made it perfectly clear that if I snitched on him and his boy, he was going to murder me and anyone close to me. And there's no way I can let that happen.

"I see you're a straight shooter." The detective said with a little bit of humor.

"I just want to answer any questions that you have for me so I can get out of here. You're not the only person I need to see while I'm in Virginia."

"Okay, well can you tell me where you were when your house caught on fire the other night?"

"I was on the road heading to Maryland."

"What time was that?"

"I don't know. Maybe 8:00, 8:30."

"What time did you get to Maryland?"

"It's a four and a half hour drive. So, I think I got there like around 12:30 or one o'clock."

"Did you stop anywhere in route to Maryland?"

I thought for a moment and then I said, "Yes, I stopped at a Mc. Donald's restaurant in Fredericksburg." I said confidently.

"Do you have a receipt that could give us that time stamp?"

"I ordered a cup of coffee in the drive thru. But I'm not sure if I still have that receipt."

"Without that receipt, we can't establish an alibi for you."

"Oh wait," I began to say while I was gathering my thoughts, "I talked a state trooper."

"Did the state trooper pull you over?"

"No. I was already parked in the parking lot of the Mc. Donald's restaurant so he got out of his car, walked over to mine and told me that my back taillight was out. He then told me to get it fixed. I told him that I would and that was it. I pulled and left."

"Did he issue you a citation?"

"No. But he did ask me for my license and registration."

"Did he give you his name?"

"No, he didn't. But I'm sure if you call the precinct in that area and ask the dispatcher who was patrolling that night, they'd give you his name." I told him. I wasn't about to let this cracker screw up my alibi because he wants to tie me to the house fire at my home. I'm not having it.

"I will look into that." He replied nonchalantly like he didn't believe a word I said. "When was the last time you spoke with your husband?" His questions continued.

"The last time I spoke with him was yesterday."

"That was the last time you spoke with him?"

"Yes,"

"What did you two talk about?"

"He called about reconciling. But I told him that I wasn't interested."

"What time was that?"

"I'm not sure. Maybe 8:00."

"Did you set your house on fire?"

"No, I didn't."

"Do you have any idea who done it?"

"I think you may need to address that question to my husband. Remember he sent someone to my house to kill me but my sister Anna was killed instead. So, maybe the same guy came back to finish the job." I replied sarcastically.

"What would you do if you find out that your husband didn't have anything to do with the house fire?"

"I wouldn't do anything but tell you that it was time to continue on with this investigation."

Detective Grantham chuckled. "If I didn't know the history of the relationships with your husband and the other couple, Leon and Charlene Bunch I would have major concerns for you."

"And what does that mean?" I became defensive.

"It means that I want you to be honest with me right now and tell me the truth about what happened at your home the other night. And who started the fire."

"What do you mean, what happened? And who started the fire? If I knew, don't you think that I would've called and told you?"

"I can't say what you would do. But I do know that if you don't tell me what happened at your home the other night, things are gonna end up really bad for me." He warned me.

"Sounds like you know something that I don't." I said, standing my ground although I was coming unraveled underneath this façade I was projecting.

"I'm waiting for the coroner to call me back with the confirmation I need, but you and I both know whose body was found burned too death in your home."

"I don't know anything." I stuck to my guns.

Detective Grantham got up a little bit and scooted his chair towards me and then he leaned forward so his face was only a few inches from mine. "Mrs. Davis, tell me why Charlene Bunch's body was found in your home?"

"Charlene Bunch?" I replied, giving off the impression that I didn't believe what he was saying.

"Yes, Charlene Bunch. We found her half-burned driver's license in her purse which was amongst the debris in the family room of your house. Now tell me what happened? And how she ended up in your home?" Detective Grantham pressed me.

"Look, I'm speechless. I'm just as surprised as you are. So, I don't know what to tell you." I answered him. But from the expression he was giving me, I could tell that he wasn't at all happy with my response.

"I'm gonna ask you one more time and if you don't give me the right answer, I won't be able to help you after I get the judge to sign off on an indictment for you." He threatened.

The sound of the word indictment shook me. At one point, I wanted to lay everything out on the table and tell the detective everything I knew. But then, I realized that if I had done that, he'd be able to charge me with accessory after the fact. Not to mention, that Kevin and his boys would come after me and kill me and my family. So, as far as I'm concerned, my best bet would be to deny everything. "Look sir, do what you gotta do because I can't tell you something that you wanna hear. I can't tell you why you found Charlene's body in my house. And I can't tell you who started the fire. But if you want my opinion, if the body you found is really Charlene's body, it wouldn't shock me if my husband sent her there to torch my place but got caught up in it herself." I told him.

"That's a good story. But that's not what happened."

"Since you got all the answers, why don't you tell me what happened?"

"Well, I think Charlene came over to confront you. You too got into an argument. Then a fight ensued. You got the best of her. You may have killed her accidently. And to cover the whole incident up, you torched your house with her in it so you could hide the evidence."

"Sorry. That didn't happen. So, try again." I said sarcastically.

"It may not have happened in that order, but it happened."

"Yeah, whatever! Tell me what happens now? Because I've told you everything I know." I responded cynically.

"Mrs. Davis, I'm trying to help you here."

"You aren't trying to help me. You're trying to get me to admit to something that I didn't do. So, if you're not placing me under arrest, then I am out of here." I said and then I stood up from my seat.

"If you walk out of this room, I won't be able to help you after I charge you with Charlene's murder and arson."

"Do what you gotta' do." I told him and then I walked out of the room.

I Made My Choice

To walk out of that interview room without handcuffs around my wrists was the most liberating feeling I had in a long time. Detective Grantham tried to back me into a corner a few times during his questioning, but thankfully, I always found a way out of it. If I hadn't, I'd been on my way to booking instead of meeting back up with my sister Karin whose been waiting for me in the lobby of this fucking police station.

I gave her a huge smile as soon as I was able to lay my eyes on her. She stood up from her chair and walked towards me. "You're done?" She asked in a hopeful manner.

"Yeah, let's get out of here." I told her and grabbed her hand. While I was pulling her towards the front glass doors of the precinct, my heart almost jumped out of my chest. "Trice, is that you?" One of the two women asked me after they walked into the lobby.

"Grand mommy, that's her. That's the lady that took me away from my mommy." The child yelled. But it wasn't just any child, it was Charlene and Leon's son.

I didn't know whether to say hello, or run out of this place as fast as I could. I wished I could've disappeared with the snap of my finger. But I couldn't so I stood there and waited for the inevitable. "Hi Mrs. Bunch, how are you?" I said.

"I'm not good at all. But, how are you? I saw on the news that you lost your sister."

"Yes, I did. But, my family and I are dealing with it as best as we can."

"Good to hear." She said and then she pointed towards the lady next to her. "This is Charlene's mother and she and I are both here to file a missing person report for Charlene." Mrs. Bunch said while Charlene's mother looked at me from head to toe. This Madea-look-a-like was giving me the evil eye.

"Oh, I'm sorry to hear that." I replied, trying to give these ladies the most sincere expression I could muster up.

"She took me to your house grand mommy." The little Leon blurted out.

"What are you talking about Lil Leon?" Mrs. Bunch asked him.

"He's saying that she was the one that took him from his mama." Charlene's mother chimed in.

I smiled. "Took him from his mama? When?" I chuckled, with the purpose of defusing any idea of connecting me to the other night when I dropped him off and left. "He must remember me when I was with his dad the day we picked him up from your house Mrs. Bunch." I continued while I said a silent prayer, hoping these two women wouldn't put two and two together. "So, you say you're down here to file a missing person report for Charlene?" I continued and looked directly at Mrs. Bunch.

"Why? Do you know where she is?" Charlene's mother blurted out.

Caught off guard by her sudden outburst, I hesitated for a second and then I looked at my sister Karin. "What kind of question is that?" My sister Karin interjected.

"Let her answer it." Charlene's mother came back.

"I'm sorry but no I don't." I finally answered her. I looked at her like she had lost her damn mind.

"Come on Betty, let's not do that here." Mrs. Bunch stepped in.

"You heard what our grandson said."

"I don't care what your grandson said. My sister didn't take him from his mama. And she doesn't know where his mother is." Karin spat. My sister wasn't holding back on Charlene's mother.

"Look, I'm not gonna stand here and listen to this mess!" I finally said. "Mrs. Bunch, I will call you later. So, take care."

"Wait, let me get your number." Mrs. Bunch replied and pulled her cellphone from her handbag. As soon as she had her phone in her hand, she programmed my number in it. "Call me anytime." I insisted and walked off with my sister Karin in tow.

Immediately after we got outside Karin said, "What was her deal?

"I don't know. But I do know that I was about to fuss that old bitch out!"

"Me too! I was gritting my teeth the whole time I was standing beside you." Karin said while we were getting back into her car.

"So, what was that kid talking about? And why was he saying that you took him from his mama?" Karin asked me as she drove out of the parking lot of the police precinct.

"Girl, I have the slightest idea. That's why I said, he probably remembered me when I was with his dad."

"Wasn't it weird to see Leon's mother and Charlene's mother?"

"What about the missing person's report?"

"What do you mean?"

"Do you really believe Charlene is missing?"

"Fuck no! Knowing that snake as bitch, she probably ran off with another man. Leon always talked about her being said a ho."

"Well then, problem solved." Karin commented. "So, where are we going now?" She continued as we took the next exit to get on the highway.

"Let's go to the Caribbean Restaurant near Lynnhaven Mall." I suggested.

"Sounds good to me." Karin stated and then she headed in that direction.

During the drive to the restaurant, Karin started asking me a ton of questions again. I really wasn't in the mood to talk considering what I just went through back at the police precinct. Not only had I been interrogated by the cop, I ran into Leon and Charlene's mother. I swear, I was a ball of nerves standing in front of those two women. But what almost sealed my fate was when Lil Leon called me out in front of his grandmothers. If Mrs. Bunch would've taken that little boy's words seriously, I'm sure she would've questioned me more. Thank God it didn't go that way.

"So, what was the detective talking about?"

"He wanted to know what time I left my house the night of the fire. And then he asked me how long it took me to drive to Maryland since that's where I told him I went."

"Does he think you started the fire?" She wanted to know.

"He insinuated a couple of times. But I told him that he needed to go down to the jail and talk to Troy because it could've been him. I mean, he was able to send someone by my house to kill me. So, why not send them to burn my house down?" I replied sarcastically.

"And what did he say?"

"Nothing but that he's gonna look into it."

"Did he find out who the lady was that they found in your house?"

"Not yet. He said, he's waiting for the coroner to call him back with that information." I lied. I couldn't tell her what the detective and I talked about. It would get back to my mother in the blink of an eye. Keeping that information close to my heart is my best bet right now. Who knows.... I may feel differently later.

Karin let out a long sigh. "Wouldn't it be weird if the person they found in your house was Charlene?"

My heart did a somersault and landed in the pit of my stomach. The hair on my arms stood up too. "Yeah, that would be, huh?" I finally answered her.

"I know I keep saying this over and over again…. But it's a shame that you have to go through all of this."

"I know. But it'll be over soon, I hope." I said.

Fuck Off

K arin and I ordered Oxtails with peas and rice for our entrée after the waitress took us to our table. While we waited for the waitress to bring our food back, Karin's cellphone started ringing. Before she answered it, she looked at the caller ID and smiled. "Oh, this is my boo calling me." She announced and then she took the call after the second ring. "Hello," she said, smiling from ear to ear.

I couldn't hear what he was saying, but I'm sure that whatever it was, Karin was enjoying everything single bit of it. So instead of eavesdropping on her call, I pulled out my cellphone and started sifting through old text messages from Troy before he went to jail.

The first message dated over two months ago, said, *Trice, I love u so much! Will u please meet up with me 2nite. I'm goin crazy ova here without u.*

100

But of course, I ignored them. But the text messages I did answer were the ones that Charlene sent to me after she found out that I was going to the prison to see Leon.

U lying 2 timing hoe! U wanna fuck up my marriage bcuz ur's is fucked up? Leave my fucking husband alone. U fuckin' home wrecka!

I text that bitch back and said, *Fuck u! U fucking tramp! U broke up your own marriage after u sucked my husband's dick. Leon didn't want u putting your lips anywhere near him after Troy came in your mouth. So fuck off u bitch!*

Immediately after I sent Charlene that text message, I blocked her from responding to me. I'm sure this pissed her off because she made it her mission to tell Troy about it. To add insult to injury, the bitch brought three killers to my house to murder me because she lied to them about some money I was supposed to have. I thank God those guys saw right through her bullshit and gave me a pass because if they hadn't my body would've been the one the cops found instead of hers.

I got to admit that that bitch was definitely a thorn in my side. So, it brings me nothing but joy that she's out of my life for good.

When the waitress brought our food to the table, Karin was still on the phone talking to her man but I made her get off the phone. "Baby, the waitress just brought us our food, so let me eat and then I'll call you back, okay?" She said and then she ended the call.

"Your man misses you already, huh?" I wondered aloud.

"Yeah, he asked me when were we coming back to Maryland. So, I told him I'll know later today." She replied and then she looked down at her plate of food. "This shit looks so!" She continued as she dug her fork into the meat covered in gravy.

"Trust me, it's mouth-watering." I commented between chews.

While Karin sunk her teeth into the tender meat of the oxtail, my cellphone started ringing. At that very moment, anxiety consumed me. I didn't want to answer my phone or look at the caller ID for that matter. I was tired of talking to people. So why won't they leave me alone? "Want me to see who it is?" Karin asked me.

"Yes, please." I replied and then I grabbed my cellphone from my purse and handed it to her.

As soon as Karin looked at the caller ID she sucked her teeth and said, "It's that fucking husband of yours."

"Wait, what are you doing?" I asked Karin after she pressed the SEND button to answer the call.

"I'm getting ready to tell this nigga that we know he had something to do with y'all house burning down."

"Don't tell him shit! Fuck him! I protested. The nerve of that nigga calling me again. I just talked to him yesterday.

"No! He's gonna hear what I gotta say." Karin insisted and then she said, "Nigga, you got a fucking nerve calling my sister. Haven't you reeked enough drama in her life?" She snapped.

I scooted my chair close to Karin so I could hear with Troy was saying. "Karin, can I please speak to my wife?" He asked her in a polite way.

"Whatcha' wanna tell her how sorry you are for having our sister Anna killed? Or are you sorry for getting somebody to burn down the fucking house?"

"Whatcha' talking about? I didn't get anybody to burn our house down." Troy yelled through the cellphone.

"Nigga stop lying!"

"Yo' Karin, I swear, I ain't get nobody to burn our house down."

"Tell that shit to the judge because the cops are investigating it. And they told Trice that if you did have something to do with it, you're gonna get charged with it. Speaking of which, the bitch you sent to burn down the house is dead too. She must've lit her own self on fire while she was trying to do your dirty deed."

"Karin, I don't know where you're getting your information from, but I ain't did shit. I just got off lockdown. So, I would really appreciate it if you let me speak to my wife." Troy begged.

Before Karin gave Troy the okay, she looked at me and whispered, "Do you wanna talk to him?"

"Give me the phone." I said and took it out of Karin's hand. "What do you want now?" I asked him.

"When I called you yesterday and asked you about the house, you told me that it wasn't burnt down. So, I left it alone. But then a few minutes ago, the jail counselor comes and pulls me out the block and tells me that I need to call some detective dude. So, the counselor gets him on the phone and hands the phone to me. And I'm like what's up? So, he goes into this spiel and ask me if I talked to you? And I say, yes. So, then he says, when? And I tell him what time it was. But when he asked me about our house getting burned down and was I involved in it? And if I knew the woman that died in that fire? I almost cursed the guy out. So, my question to you is, why did you lie to me when I asked you about it yesterday?"

"I don't have to answer that."

"Why not? That's my house too. And besides, a fucking woman died in there. So, why you feel like you don't have to answer me? Do you know that cop is probably trying to find a way to link me to that bullshit!?"

"Why don't you just fess up to it and ask him if he could tie all your charges together and make a plea deal? If you're lucky, you may walk away with 100-years!" I commented sarcastically. I knew Troy had nothing to do with Charlene's death, but who cares? He was responsible for my sister's death so I have no sympathy for him. I hope Detective Grantham does charge him with the house fire and Charlene's death. Troy is an animal and animals belong in cages.

"So, it's like that?"

"Yep."

"Damn! I never thought shit would get like this between us."

"Are you done?"

"No, I'm not."

"Well, I am. And I'm moving on. So, why don't you just leave me alone?" I advised him.

"Trice I am so sorry for taking you through all the stuff you've been going through, but I would swear on a stake of bibles that I never put a hit out on you and I didn't get someone to burn down our house. I love you with all my heart!"

"Yeah, yeah, yeah… save that for your next wife because I'm moving on. And so you know, as soon as the insurance company cut the check for the house, I will send your half to you." I told him and then I pressed the end button.

"Damn! You aren't taking no shit from him, huh?" Karin commented after I disconnected Troy's call and dropped my cellphone back into my purse.

"Karin, I am over him and whoever else that wants to cause harm and turmoil in my life. I just wanna be happy. That's it."

"With that attitude sis, you will get it too." Karin assured me and then we started eating our food again.

Why Now?

I'm just now realizing that my eyes are bigger than my stomach. I thought I would be able to finish my entire lunch, but my gut failed me. "Can I get a to-go container?" I asked the young Jamaican chick that waited on us.

"Yeah, me too." Karin said and pushed her plate to the side.

The young woman returned to our table and handed us both a white, Styrofoam container and placed our check next to it. I guess Karin was feeling good because she paid for both of our food. "Feeling generous today?" I said and smiled at her.

She chuckled. "Don't get used to it. I'm just doing it today." She replied as she scrapped the food from her plate and into the Styrofoam container.

"Thanks for giving me noticed." I chuckled a little while poured my food into my container as well.

On our way out of the restaurant my cellphone started ringing again. Now my nerves were already frazzled because of the interviews I had earlier with the detective and the fire inspector, so when my phone rang it gave me an unsettling feeling. I dreaded to look at the caller ID but I did it anyway. Karin looked over at me while she started the ignition. "It's probably mama." She said.

"Nah, it's not her. But, I wish it was." I said and then I pressed down on the SEND button. "Hello."

"Hi Trice honey, this is Mrs. Bunch." Hearing this lady's voice caused my stomach to rumble with fear. Not knowing the reason why she was calling me began to make me feel uneasy, so I pressed my hand against my chest and waited to hear what she had to say.

"Hi Mrs. Bunch. What's going on?" I asked casually.

"I know when we ran into each other earlier, we didn't get to talk like I wanted to so I was wondering would you come by my house later?"

I hesitated for a second and then I said, "What's this about?"

"I really don't wanna say over the phone." She replied and then she said, "You do remember where I live, right?"

Wait! Hold up. That was not a great response for me. And what does she mean, do I still know where she lives? Was that a trick question? For all I know this old lady could be setting me up. Not only that, what does she mean she doesn't want to talk about it over the phone? What could be so secretive? Now, I didn't want to seem like a bitch, so I compromised with her. "Why don't you meet me at a Starbucks near the mall?" I suggested.

"I wish I could but I just got in the house and changed my clothes."

No, this bitch didn't! She calls me and ask me to come by her house so she could talk to me and when I ask her to meet me half way she tries to play me like I owe her something. I don't wanna talk to her. She wants to talk to me. So, what's her problem? Is she crazy? I mean, the only thing I can think of is that she wants to set me up. She did just come from the police precinct so maybe Detective Grantham is trying to use her to get me to confess about knowing what really happened to Charlene. But I'm not dumb. I have plenty of sense. And if she doesn't, that's on her not me.

"Mrs. Bunch, I'm sorry but I don't have that type of time. My house just burned down and I've got a lot of running around to do." I began to explain but she interjected.

"Oh yeah, I heard about that." She acknowledged.

"When did you hear about it?" I asked her. The sudden mention of my house set off alarms in my head. She didn't mention it earlier when she saw me. So, I need to know who was the source of that information.

"I just saw it in the newspaper." She quickly answered.

But I knew that was bullshit because her son Leon and I used to talk about her ass all the time. And one of the things that he told me about her was that she hated reading newspapers. She complained about how the local newspaper used a smaller font than what they used to use. Moral of the story is, Mrs. Bunch was a TV girl and has been that way for a few years now.

"When did you see it?" I pressed the issue.

"I picked one up from the market on my way home."

"Mrs. Bunch, I'm sorry but I'm not gonna be able to make it. If you wanna talk to me you're gonna have to meet me at the Starbucks."

She paused for a second and then she said, "Well, I guess I could put my clothes back on. Can you be there in like an hour?"

I looked down at my wrist watch. "Yes, one hour is perfect." I told her.

"All right, well I'll see you then." She replied and then we both disconnected the call.

"This bitch thinks I'm fucking stupid." I spat and stuffed my cellphone down into my purse.

"What just happened?" Karin inquired.

Before I answered Karin, I thought about what I could tell her that wouldn't contradict what she and I had already discussed concerning my house fire and the fact that I knew whose body was found amongst the ashes. I figured that if I could keep those two elements out of the discussion then I'd be fine. "She wants me to meet up with her so see can talk to me."

"What for?" Karin's questions continued as she pulled out on the main road.

"She wouldn't say."

"Do you have an idea why?"

"I'm thinking she may wanna talk about her son. But then again, I'm not sure."

"Are you going?"

"Nope."

"Then where are we going?"

"To see an attorney."

"Why?"

"Because I think I'm gonna need one." I told her and then I turned my attention towards the clouds in the sky. "God, if you hear me, please take control of this situation before it gets any uglier. Only you can do it." I whispered so Karin couldn't hear me. I can't afford to put anything in her head right now.

Talk to my Attorney

From the time I got off the phone with Mrs. Bunch, I started Googling local attorneys. I was about to call the attorney that was representing Troy but when I realized that it would be a conflict of interest, I went down the list to the next one. "Have you found one yet?" Karin wanted to know. She complained about driving around in circles a little while ago, so I told her to pull over on the side of the street until I locate one.

"I think I have." I said after I dialed the number to an attorney by the name of Jerry Mane, Esq., whose office was only a couple of blocks away. And from reading his list of credentials, he had enough experience to fend off Detective Grantham and any other cop that worked down at that precinct. The fact that they were using Mrs. Bunch to get information out of me was my cue that I needed to protect myself. "Nato, Mane and Shapiro." A woman answered.

"Hi, my name is Trice Davis and I would like to speak with Jerry Mane, if he's available." I replied while I held my cellphone against my ear.

"He's with a client right now. But I'm certain I could get him to call you back if you leave me your name and number." The woman said.

"Well, I really want to make an appointment with him if I can."

"Sure. When would you like to come in?"

"Today, if that's possible."

"Okay, hold on a minute. Let me check to see if he has an opening. I'll be right back." She told me and then everything went radio silent.

"Does he have an opening?" Karin asked.

"She told me to hold on," I began to explain but then the lady came back on the line and said, "Okay, you're in luck. Mr. Mane has a 5 o'clock appointment left so if that works for you, then I'll pencil you in."

"Yes, pencil me in." I told her. "Hey but wait, is there a consultation fee?"

"No there isn't."

"Okay. Great. See you then."

Immediately after I ended the call with the lady at the firm, Karin didn't hesitate to ask me where we were going. "My appointment with the lawyer isn't until five so take me back over to my house."

"To do what?"

"Can you just do what I tell you to do instead of always asking me a bunch of questions?"

"I'm family. And I love you so I should be able to ask you any question I want." Karin replied sarcastically.

"Girl please, you're talking out the side of your neck." I told her while I was sifting through my text messages on my phone.

"You can call it what you want. But remember I'm driving and I will drop you off on the side of the road if I want to." Karin chuckled as she maneuvered in and out of the busy traffic.

"Well okay driver, drive me to my house please." I came back at her.

She chuckled again and slapped me on the thigh in a playful manner. Karin was a sweetheart and I know she loves me no matter what, which is why it's hard for me to keep her in the dark about what was really going on in my chaotic life. I just hope and pray that I can defuse this whole thing before it blows up in my face.

Seeing Things

I've never heard a woman complain so much in my life. I literary had to pull tooth and nail to stop Karin from griping about walking around certain parts of my house with me. "That fire-line-do-not-cross tape is wrapped around the trees and your house for a reason. And that reason is to keep people like you and me from walking around it." She protested.

"Oh, stop crying. I told you I only need five minutes to look through this rubble." I tried reasoning with her while I carefully walked across the ashes and debris from the fire.

"Do you realize that some of this debris is still hot?" She pointed out.

"Of course, I do. Why else would I be hopping around?" I replied and then something caught my attention. I took a few steps and then I reached down and grabbed a book that was located at the back of my house. It was a photo

117

album. One of the five albums Troy and I collected over the years we've been married. After I had it in my hands I brushed it off a little and then I opened it. "Is that a photo album?" Karin asked while peering over my right shoulder.

"Yeah, it is. This is the one I filled up with all the pictures Troy and I took on every anniversary we had." I retorted as I turned the half-burnt pages. I noticed some of the pages were melted togethers while the other pages were burned completely.

"I hate sounding negative, but seeing this photo album destroyed like this should send a clear message that it wasn't meant for y'all to be together."

I looked back at Karin. "You sure know when to say some fucked up shit!"

"It ain't fucked up. It's the truth."

Instead of feeding into Karin's catty ways, I walked away from her and continued looking through the rubble. Karin started walking behind me but then she stopped. "I didn't know you wore Michael Kors shoes." She said as she picked up a sneaker from the pile of ashes. I turned around in a flash and zoomed in on the shoe. "Oh, wait, this is too smile for you.

Think it belonged to the lady that the firefighter found?"

I wanted to puke when I saw Karin holding Charlene's shoe in her hand. I can't believe what I was seeing. So, I rushed back over to where Karin was standing and knocked the shoe out of her hands. "What did you do that for?" She spat while she gave me this evil off expression.

"I don't want you putting your finger prints or DNA on it." I lied. I knocked it out of her hands to prevent her from putting two and two together and figure out who really owns that shoe. "Come on and let's get out of here." I instructed her and gave her a friendly push in front of me. As she walked away ahead of me, I snatched Charlene's shoe up from the ashes and stuck it down in the waistline of my pants. I even kicked the debris around with my feet to see if I could find the other one but I couldn't so I walked through the rubble and followed Karin towards the car. By the time I made it on the sidewalk in front of my home, I saw a black car coming towards me. Instead of trying to make it across the street to Karin's car, I stood there curbside, allowing the car to go ahead of me. Now as the tinted window vehicle came within a couple of feet of me, it began to slow down. I let out a long sigh. "What the fuck are you doing? I ain't got all day." I said. But as the car came closer, I realized that this car was a black, 4-door Dodge Charger. "Oh my God! It's the fucking detective." I mumbled to myself. "Shit! He's coming here to arrest me and take me to jail. Not to mention, that I've got Charlene's shoe stashed underneath my clothes. Shit! Shit! Shit!" I continued talking to myself.

While I waited for the inevitable; the cop pulling up to the curb, hop out of his unmarked car and arrest me, I closed my eyes and counted backwards from five to zero. Immediately after I started the countdown in my head, the first thing I heard was the car coming to a complete stop. After that, I heard the power window coming down. When I got down to number two I heard a man's voice say, "You're a hard person to find."

Taken aback by the man's voice, I opened my eyes and got the shock of my life. "It's you." I said, not knowing what to say.

"Yeah, it's me. And I'm here to let you know that the word on the streets is the cops know that somebody set your crib on fire. So, I'm here to remind you that if I find out that you're running your fucking mouth I'm gonna kill everyone you love. You understand?"

"Yes, I understand completely." I assured him.

"Good. Well, look both ways before you cross the street." He instructed me and then he pulled off.

Without hesitation on my part, I sprinted across the street to Karin's car as soon as the tail of Kevin's car passed me. "Who was that?" Karin asked me as soon as I got into her car and closed the door shut.

"Some guy trying to flirt with me." I lied while I snapped my seat belt in place.

"Oh nah! Somethings wrong."

"What do you mean?" I tried to remain calm.

"Bitch, you haven't wore your seat belt since we left Maryland. But now you wanna put it on?" Karin pointed out as she searched my face for an answer.

"Look, I'm just ready to get out of here. The sight and condition of my house has dampened my mood. That's all." I lied once again.

Karin sat there and looked at me for another couple of seconds and then she said, "I think you're holding something back from me. And I'm gonna figure it out by the end of the day."

"Girl, there's nothing wrong. I just wanna get out of here. So, let's go please." I continued and I sat forward in my seat.

Karin made a few more comments about my sudden condition of nervousness after she pulled away from my house. I didn't entertain any of it, because I had other pressing stuff on my mind. Staying alive was the most important one. And keeping her and my other family members alive was the second most important thing. End of story.

Call Me Crazy

The ride to the attorney's office only took us a little under twelve minutes to get there. I tried to convince Karin to stay in the car, but she wasn't having it. "You're not leaving me in the car for God knows how many hours. But, I'll wait in the lobby area." She reasoned.

I didn't make a fuss about her waiting in the lobby area of the attorney's office so immediately after we entered the building, she took at seat a few feet away from the receptionist's desk while I checked in. "I'm here to see Jerry Mane." I told the young, Caucasian woman behind the desk. She looked to be every bit of 23-years old, so I assumed that she was straight out of college. Plus, she looked like she was free spirited. God knows what I would pay to swap shoes with her.

While I waited to be called back to the attorney's office, I sat in a chair next to Karin.

And as soon as I sat down she said, "What is that sticking out around your waist?"

She had no idea that I picked Charlene's shoe back up from the ground after she walked. So, when she poked at it and couldn't figure out what it was, she instantly lifted my shirt. I swear, I was mortified when she saw what it was. "Is that the same shoe you knocked out of my hand?" She questioned me.

I immediately felt like a fucking kid who'd just got caught stealing from her parent. I didn't know how to respond to her. So, I covered the shoe back up with my shirt and tried my best to ignore her but she wasn't having it. "Trice why the fuck are you hiding that shoe underneath your shirt?" She asked me. I knew she wasn't going to let this conversation go without me giving her a good explanation.

I took a deep breath and then I exhaled. "Look, it's not what you think." I finally said in a low whisper.

"What do you mean it's not what I think? I'm not thinking anything, which is why I'm trying to get you to tell me what's going on." Karin replied in a low like whisper too.

"I brought the shoe with me so I can give it to the lawyer." I told her. But that was also a lie. I just hoped that she would believe it.

"Trice, that's bullshit and you know it. You know I know when you're lying. So, fess up and tell me the real reason why you got that burnt up shoe hidden underneath your clothes? I mean, look how filthy it is. I can even smell it."

"Mrs. Davis, Mr. Mane can see you now." The receptionist announced.

Yes, saved by the bell. I thought to myself and then I stood up on my feet.

Karin was pissed. But I couldn't concern myself with her right now. I've got other shit to do and hiring this lawyer to keep me out of jail, is what I've got to focus on. Hopefully, by the time I come out of this meeting, I would've thought of a good explanation about why I've got Charlene's shoe hidden underneath my clothes. Or, Karin won't be so angry with me. Either way, I've got to get my ducks in a row.

"You better be ready to answer my question when you come back out here." Karin warned me. I ignored her and proceeded to the back.

When I entered into Mr. Mane's office, he stood up behind his deck, extended his hand and greeted me. "How are you Mrs. Davis?" He asked me.

"Not too good." I replied.

"Have a seat." He insisted.

I took a seat in one of the chairs placed in front of his desk like he instructed me to and then he went straight into question mode. "So, what brings you here?"

Mr. Mane was a tall, slender, Caucasian man with a flair for dressing really nice. His tailor-made suit, Gucci cufflinks and Rolex watch was a clear indication that he made a nice living, defending his clients in a court of the law. "I'm not sure if you know, but my house was torched in a fire a couple nights ago. And while the firemen were putting the fire out, they found a woman's body amongst the ash and rubble."

"Oh yeah, I heard about that." He interjected. "Was the woman related to you?" He continued.

"No, she wasn't. And that's why I'm here."

"Okay, keep going." He insisted.

"Well, the night my house caught on fire, I was on the highway driving back to Maryland. But the next day, I get a call from Detective Grantham telling me that he needed me to come back to town so he and the fire and arson investigator could have an interview with me. So, I did. I saw the fire investigator first and then I stopped by the precinct to see the detective. But five minutes into the interview he started

126

accusing me of starting the fire and tries to get me to say that I had something to do with the woman they found amongst the ashes and debris. So, I told him he was crazy and walked out of there."

"Why do you think the detective pointed the finger at you?"

"I don't know."

"Did he tell you who the woman was?"

"He mentioned her name."

"What was her name?"

"Charlene Bunch."

"Would you happen to know her?"

"Yes, I know who she is."

"And how do you know her?"

"She was married to my husband's friend."

"Where is her husband?"

"He's deceased."

"When did he pass away?"

"A few weeks ago."

"Did she have any other connection to you besides being married to your husband's friend?"

"Yes, she fucked my husband. So, I fucked her husband."

"Oh okay, I see where this is going now." He said. "So, does the detective know the backstory?

"Yes, he does."

"Okay, I can see why he tried to back you into a corner. So, let me ask you, has anyone besides your husband and her husband seen you guys have confrontation in public?"

"No. But we've cursed each other out via text messages."

"Have you ever threatened to kill her? You know, via text message or voicemail messages?"

"No. Never."

"Okay, good."

"Well, here's the big question," he said and then he paused, "how can you explain her being in your home and dying there as a result of a fire?"

"I don't know. I didn't put her there."

"I understand that. But, you may have to answer that question in front of a judge."

Getting frustrated by what the attorney was telling me, I started shaking my head, like I wasn't feeling him or the shit he was saying. "Listen Mrs. Davis, if you say you don't know how she got there, then that's what it is. But if I come on as your attorney, then I'm gonna need your full cooperation. And I'm gonna need you to be brutality honest with me."

"And I would." I assured him.

"Okay great, so for starters, I'm gonna forbid you from talking to any law enforcement officers as of this very moment. If Detective Grantham calls you and wants to speak with you, tell him you'd been advised by your attorney that he can no longer speak with you when I'm not present. And if he tries to give you a hard time, then give him my number and I will handle it from there."

"All right, I can do that. So, what is your retainer and how much do you charge by the hour?"

"For you, my retainer is $1,000. And I charge $150 an hour. Think you can swing that?"

"I'm gonna get my mom to help me, so I should be fine."

"Sounds great. So, pay my receptionist on your way out and have her to give you my card. Use it to call me any time you need to."

I stood up on my feet. "Thank you so much! I feel better now after talking to you." I told him and shook his hand.

"That's what I am here for." He replied and then he escorted me out to the hallway. "Take care."

"I will. And thanks again."

When I entered back into the reception area, Karin was front and center. I glanced at her and she gave me the look of death. I knew then that she was still upset with me and then I was going to have some serious explaining after we leave out of this law firm.

"Mr. Mane told me to give you my retainer." I told the reception.

"How much am I supposed to be accepting from you?"

"One thousand dollars."

"Are you paying cash or card?"

"My credit card." I said as I handed her my Visa.

I watched her as she swiped my card through her credit card machine. She pressed a few buttons and then she handed me my card back. A couple of seconds later, the machine spewed out my receipt. "Here sign this one and this one here is your copy." She pointed out.

After I signed her copy, I took my copy and stuffed it down into my handbag. "Have a nice day." She said.

"Thanks. You do the same." I replied and headed to the exit door.

I saw Karin staring at me through my peripheral vision. I also so the steam coming from her ears like she train. "Are you ready to tell me what the fuck is going on?" She hissed.

"Can you wait at least until we get in the car?" I spat. I know she means well and wants to know what's going on with me, but there's a time and a place for that.

"Okay. But as soon as we get in the car, I want you to tell me everything fucking thing!" She was livid.

Immediately after she and I climbed into the car, she started up the ignition and sped out of the parking lot of the firm like she was a Nascar driver. And as soon as we stopped at the first STOP sign, she turned her head around and looked straight at me. "Trice, tell me right now, what's going on?"

I took the shoe from underneath my shirt and sat it on the floor in front of me. "You gotta promise me that you won't say anything to mama. Your boyfriend either."

"What is it?"

"Karin, you've gotta promise me first. Because what I'm about to tell you is serious."

"Wait, you're scaring me Trice."

"Just promise me." I pressured her. I needed to know that she was going to keep her mouth closed.

"Okay. I promise." She finally agreed.

I took a deep breath and then I exhaled. "This Michael Kors shoe belongs to Charlene." I started off saying but Karin cut me off.

Shocked by my answer, Karin looked at me like she was about to have a panic attack. "Wait, you're talking about Charlene, Charlene? The one that y'all did the wife swap with?"

"Yes," I said.

After I answered Karin's question she slowed the car down and then she pulled it over on the side of the road. Once she had the car in park, she turned and faced me. "How do you know that that's Charlene's shoe?"

"Because I saw her the night of the fire."

"Where did you see her?"

"She was in my house. Her, her son and three other guys were in my house."

"What the fuck are you talking about Trice? Why were they in your house?"

"When I left mama's house the other night so I come home, clean up and take care other things concerning the house, I walked through the front door and found Charlene, her son Lil Leon and three other guys sitting in there waiting on me."

"Are you fucking kidding me?"

"No."

"How did they get in your house? And why were they there?"

"I don't know how they got into my house. But the reason they were there waiting on me was because Charlene told them that I was sitting on $10,000 from the reality show but the money belonged to Leon. And somehow Leon owed them money so they figured the only way they'd be able to get it is if they got it from me. Unfortunately for them, I didn't have the money. And when I told the ring leader, whose name was Kevin, that Charlene lied to them, they beat her up really bad while her son sat there and watched. Towards the end, the guy Kevin told me that he was going to let me go but that I had to take Charlene's son with me and I had to promise not to tell anyone what happened because he was going to kill her and leave her body in my house while they torch it and let it burn to the ground. So, after I agreed not to say anything, I grabbed the little boy by his hand and walked out of there."

"So, wait… now this makes sense," Karin said and then she paused, "when that little boy said that you took him from his mommy, that's what he was talking about?" She continued.

"Yes, I rode around town for about thirty minutes trying to figure out where I could take him and then Leon's mom popped up in my mind, so I drove over there. As soon as I pulled up to the curb in front of her house, Lil Leon opened the back door, jumped out of the car and ran up to the front door. He knocked on the front door and a few minutes later, Mrs. Bunch opened it. But before she got a chance to see who had dropped him off, I pulled off."

"Oh my God! I can't believe you just told me all of that."

"Well, believe it. And remember that car that slowed down in front of my house when I was trying to cross the street to get back in the car with you?"

"Yes,"

"That was the nigga who killed Charlene."

"Fuck! What did he say?"

"He told me that he heard a few people in the streets saying that I was cooperating with the cops to help them with Charlene's murder. And if he finds out that it's true, he said that he's going to kill me an anyone connected to me."

"What did you say?"

"I told 'em it was a lie."

"Damn, I can't believe that Charlene's killer was in that car a few yards from me and I didn't know it. That's fucking scary!"

"No, what's scary is that he told me he was gonna be watching me."

"Trice, I know you don't want to, but you're gonna have to tell the cops what you just told me."

"Are you fucking out of your mind? I can't tell the cops shit!" I roared. Karin wasn't thinking realistically. If I told the cops what I knew, they'd arrest me for sure.

"So, then what are you going to do?"

"I don't know."

"Does the attorney know what you just told me?"

"No."

"Well, you know you're gonna have to tell him."

"I'm not telling him shit!"

"So, what are you going to do about this situation?"

"I don't know. But, I'll figure it out soon enough.

Whose Turn Is It Now

I sat there in the passenger seat of Karin's car and told her everything. I didn't leave one thing out. But it seemed like I had made a mistake doing so. She sat in the driver seat and started looking over her shoulders and in the rearview mirror, wondering were we being followed and watched right now. "Think he's watching and following us now?" She panicked.

"No, I don't think so."

"How do you know?"

"Look Karin, I don't know. But I'm still gonna need you calm down. We're gonna get through this. Okay?"

"Okay." Karin agreed.

"Let's switch seats." I insisted.

"What do you mean?"

"I'm gonna drive." I told her as I opened the passenger side door.

Instead of getting out of the car, Karin climbed over the arm rest and into the passenger seat. She closed the passenger side door while I walked around the back of the car. Immediately after I climbed into the driver seat, I closed the door and took off in the direction of my bank so I could get some cash from the ATM.

The drive to the bank was quiet. I was surprised that Karin didn't utter one word. And she didn't say anything after I almost rear ended a car that was driving extremely slow in front of me. I knew then that our trip here in Virginia was about to come to an end.

When I arrived at the bank I opted at the last minute to go inside instead of getting money from the ATM. "I'll be right back." I told her and then I exited the car.

Surprisingly, the bank wasn't crowed when I walked into the lobby. In fact, there were only two other customers and they were already being helped by other tellers, so I was immediately called to the next available teller. "How can I help you?" The black female teller asked me.

"I wanna make a withdrawal." I replied as I retrieved my driver's license from my purse. After I grabbed ahold of it, I handed it to her. She took a look at it and then she handed it back to me.

"How much are you looking to take out?" she wanted to know.

"Five hundred dollars."

"Sure, let me process your request." She told me and then she started tapping away at the keys on her computer keyboard. While she was processing my withdrawal request I looked around at my surroundings just to make sure that there wasn't anyone watching me.

"Has it been this quiet the whole day?" I asked, making small talk. I needed to do something to take my mind off everything that has transpired today.

"Yes, it has. But it'll pick around 4 o'clock when people are able to leave work."

"Okay, that makes sense." I said.

"All right, so here's your $500." She told me as she counted the money in front of me. I picked up the stack of $50's and $20's from the metal counter, thanked her and then I exited the bank.

"I'm back." I announced to Karin after I opened the car door and slid back into the driver seat.

"If you and Trice don't call the detectives that's working the case, I'm gonna do it for you." I heard my mother say and that's when I realized that Karin was on the phone with her and she had the call on speaker.

"Mom, Trice is back in the car." Karin said, acting like she was trying to do damage control. But it was too late. I knew at the moment, Karin had done the unthinkable. She broke the promise she gave me by telling our mother about Charlene's murder.

"You have such a big mouth!" I gritted my teeth at Karin.

"Trice don't be mad at your sister. She loves you and wants to look out for you." My mother chimed in pretending to be a mediator.

"Mom, I don't wanna hear it. You have no idea what you're talking about!" I spat. I was getting irritated by every word she was uttering from her mouth. My mother nor Karin knew what those guys were capable of doing. For God's sake, Kevin had just threatened to kill me if I opened my fucking mouth not even an hour ago. Sorry to say that I fucked that up.

"Trice, I'm so sorry." Karin tried apologizing. But I wasn't trying to hear it. She betrayed me and it didn't take her long to do it. I mean, damn! I had just left her alone for five minutes.

"Trice don't be mad at your sister." My mother said.

"Mom, I don't wanna hear another word from you or Karin. So, please leave me alone and stop talking about it." I huffed.

"Trice, you need to call the detective that's working this case. Because if you don't, you could be charged as an accessory." My mother warned me.

"Mom, shut up! You don't know what you're talking about! Those guys that killed Charlene are heartless. So, if they found out that I called the cops on them, they will try to kill me, you and Karin. So, leave me alone about it!" I roared.

Frustrated by the whole idea of my mother knowing about what happened and the fact that she wants me to go to the cops about it, made my blood boil. I was also feeling another panic attack coming on. Anxiety was consuming me at a rapid pace. "Karin honey, are you still there?" My mother questioned Karin.

"Yes mom, I'm still here." Karin replied, while she watched my every move.

"What is Trice doing?" My mother's questions continued.

"She's just sitting in the driver seat." Karin explained.

"Trice, would you feel better if I called the detective and told him what Karin told me?" My mother tried to reason. But her words sent me over the edge. I had become extremely angry now.

"You know what?! Fuck this!" I screamed and then I pushed open the car door and climbed back out of the driver seat.

"What's happening?" I heard my mother yell. But before Karin could answer her, I had already closed the driver side door.

Unaware about what I was going to do next, I started walking in the opposite direction of Karin's car. I wanted to get away from her as quickly as I could. Not only had she betrayed me, she also put us in danger by opening her fucking mouth to our mother. Kevin and his boys have already demonstrated to me that they would take the lives of anyone that compromises their status in the streets. I don't know those guys personally, but the way they got rid of

Charlene, I know their actions aren't to be taken lightly.

I think I walked a quarter of a mile before Karin came looking for me. So, when she pulled up on me, she powered the passenger side window down and started apologizing to me about betraying my trust. "Trice, I am so sorry for telling mom what you told me. I know I fucked up. But I was scared and needed to talk to someone else besides you."

"I understand all of that. But I told you how those guys were didn't I?" I pointed out while I walked alongside her car.

"Yes, you did. And that's why I got scared."

"Do you know that if the shoe was on the other foot, I would've kept my word with you?"

"Yes, and that's why I feel so bad. So, please forgive me." Karin pressed the issue.

I thought for a second or two while I walked alongside Karin's slow moving car. And then I stopped and faced her. "Okay, I'm gonna give you another chance. But, if you fuck that up then I'm done with you. Deal?"

"Yes, deal!" She agreed.

I'm Over It

K arin put me back in the driver seat when I got back in the car. And before I could pull off, my cellphone started ringing again. I looked at the caller ID and noticed it was Mrs. Bunch. "Who is it?" Karin wanted to know.

"It's Leon's mother."

"Are you going to answer it?"

"Fuck no!" I replied and dropped my phone into my purse.

"So, where are we on our way to now?" Karin asked.

"To the insurance company so I can file my claim." I proudly spoke.

"Well, let's go."

I didn't necessarily have to go to the insurance company to file my claim, but I did it anyway. I felt like if I went in person that I could get the ball rolling a little faster. Getting money from the house would definitely come in handy, now that I'm moving back to Maryland. And the fact that I won't have any bills while I was living with my mother would allow me to save up a nice piece of change just in case I wanna get my own place.

Having your own place has its advantages. And living with your parents has its advantages too. In reality, I just wanna be happy. So, if I move back to Maryland tomorrow and then decide to move to D.C. a month from then, then so be it. It's my life and I intend to look out of numero UNO.

Karin came inside the building with me without me telling her to do so. I noticed her looking over her shoulders the entire walk from the car and into the building. "You okay?" I whispered after we got onto the elevator.

There was a woman on the elevator with us so Karin whispered back to me. "Yeah, I'm all right." But I knew that she wasn't.

Karin was a passive type of chick. She wasn't used to all the drama of people shooting and killing each other. And the only reason why I'm somewhat numb to it is because the people who's been shot and killed in front of me deserved it.

When the elevator door opened, Karin and I walked off. "I think the office is on the right." I pointed after the elevator door opened.

"Yeah, I see it." Karin said and we both walked towards the glass door.

Like the police precinct, the insurance company waiting area had a receptionist sitting behind the desk. This time I was greeted by a black woman, that looked to be in her early 30's. She was one of those afro-centric types with long dread locks pinned up on the top of her head with some of it drooped down on the side. "Hi there," she said.

"Hi," I started off, "I'm here to file a claim for my home. It was burnt down in a fire a couple days ago." I continued.

"Do you have the police report and a report from the fire department indicating that this in fact happened? She asked me.

"No, but I spoke with the fire and arson investigator a couple of hours ago at my house. He did an interview with me too."

"Okay, I see. Well, we can start the paperwork now, but it won't go to a claims officer until we have a police and fire and arson report."

"Well, can I give you their names and then they can send the reports to you?"

"I'm sorry but it doesn't work like that."

"So, how do I get the ball rolling because I'm leaving to go back to Maryland later today?"

"The way things work now is, you can call over the phone and start your claim there. Immediately after you give us all the information we need to file the claim, you will get a claims number and then we'll go from there."

"So, I can't do anything today?" I wanted clarity.

"You can, but it won't speed up the process." The woman replied.

I let out a long sigh. "Okay. Thank you!" I said and then I turned around and left.

Back in the car Karin wanted to know what else was on the agenda for today. "I guess we can head back to Maryland." I told her after I started the ignition.

"Good, because I'm ready to get out of here." She commented.

It felt good to see the light in my sister's face. I knew she was petrified of hanging around here, so it was a no-brainer to get back on the road and take her away from this place as fast as I could.

Loyalty Over Everything

"I am so glad that we're leaving this place." Karin stated as we drove away from the insurance company.

"I knew you would be." I commented.

"So, what are we going to do with this shoe?" Karin asked me as she pointed to it. It was still on the floor from when I dropped it there.

"I'm gonna throw it over the Jordan Bridge when we cross it."

"Good, because I'm tired of looking at it." Karin chuckled and then she turned her attention to the bird in the sky. "Have you ever wished that you could fly?" She asked me.

"Yes, I have. I used to think about it a lot when I was in elementary school. And when I got into middle school, I thought about it then too. I think all that flying stuff left my system when I became an adult. But the way things are looking for me now, I sure could use a pair of wings to fly out of here and never look back."

Karin chuckled. "I'll second that." She said while she continued to watch the birds fly around in the sky.

"We're coming up on the bridge now." I announced.

Karin sat up straight in her seat. "Oh my God! This bridge is so high. It looks like we're riding on a rollercoaster."

"Yeah, it does." I smiled. And then I turned on the hazard lights.

"What are you getting ready to do?"

"I'm gonna pull the car to the side of the bridge wall and then I'm gonna get out and drop the shoe into the water."

"I don't think that's gonna be a good idea." Karin said as she looked through the side view mirror.

"Why you say that?"

"Because there are cops right behind us." She told me.

Before I could bring the car to a halt, the police officer turned on his siren. "Oh shit!" I panicked.

"See, why did you have to pull over on the bridge? He's gonna give us a fucking ticket now."

"Just calm down. I'm gonna be the one to get the ticket. Not you!" I told her while I watched both police officers get out of the patrol car.

"What if they arrest us?"

"Arrest us for what? We haven't done anything wrong. So, stop acting all freaking paranoid." I spat. Karin was really working on my last nerve. She was getting nervous for nothing.

My window was already down when the cop approached my side of the car. He was a big, white, navy seal looking dude. "Can I get your license and registration?" He asked me.

While I was getting my license from my wallet, Karin was retrieving the car registration from the glove compartment. "The car belongs to me." Karin announced to the cop on my side of the car as she passed the document on to me.

"Did we do something wrong?" Karin asked the police officer on her side of the car. He was another big, white guy that looked like he served as a navy seal. "Just cooperate with my partner and everything will be fine." He replied.

"Sir, can you tell me what's going on?" I asked him. I wanted some answers. But he ignored me. He looked down at my ID and said, "Trice Davis, will you please step out of the car."

My heart sunk into the pit of my stomach when he asked me to get out of the car. For the life of me, I couldn't figure out why this man was bothering us. Karin and I hadn't broken any laws. So, what could this be about? "Am I being arrested?" I didn't hesitate to ask. I had a fucking lawyer now and he needs to know what is going on.

"Just get out the car ma'am and follow me to my squad car." He told me.

"Ma'am, I'm gonna need you to step out of the car too." The other officer instructed Karin.

Doing as we were told, both Karin and I stepped out of her car and followed both officers back to their patrol car. They didn't waste any time putting handcuffs on us and putting us in the back of their fucking police car. And after they closed the door on us, Karin looked at me and started crying. When I saw the first tear fall from her eyes, I felt so bad. "What are they arresting us?" She sobbed.

I wanted to wipe the tears from her eyes but both of my hands were handcuffed behind my back so all I could do was console her with words. "It's just a big misunderstanding. So, please stop crying." I begged her.

"If it's all just a misunderstanding then why are they searching my car?" Her tears were falling uncontrollably now.

I looked through the front windshield and before I could blink my eye good, I saw the police officer on the passenger side of the car standing straight up, dangling Charlene's burnt shoe in the air, apparently showing it off to his partner who was on the driver side going through my purse. "Why the fuck is he going through my purse?" I yelled. But no one could hear me but Karin.

"Screw your purse! What about Charlene's shoe? How are we going to explain that?" Karin screamed at me.

"I'm just gonna tell them that I took it from my house because I wanted to conduct my own investigation." I said. I knew it was a lie but I figured that if I sold it to them, they'd buy it.

"They aren't gonna believe that crap."

"If you just let me talk to them then they won't have any other choice but to believe me."

"Yeah, okay. Good luck with that." Karin replied sarcastically and then she turned her attention towards the sky again. "This is one of those times where I wished I could fly away." She continued as the tears dropped down her face.

"Karin, I know you don't wanna hear this now, but I promise you that we're gonna be alright. They have nothing on us. We haven't done anything wrong." I tried reassuring her. I thought my words would make Karin stop crying but it didn't. I felt so badly looking at her cry her heart out and it was all because of me. I knew the only way she would stop crying is if I took full accountability, regardless of whatever it, just as long as they let her go.

While I sat in the back seat of the police car, listening to Karin sob, I started going over scenarios in my head about what I was going to say to these bastards once they decide that they want to talk. But then it dawned on me that I didn't have to say shit to them. Once I paid Mr. Jerry Mane his retainer, he officially became my counsel. And the quicker I tell these morons that, the faster they'll realized that I wasn't to be fucked with.

Judging from the time on the clock in the dashboard of the police car, Karin and I has been sitting in the back of this car for five to ten minutes before the cop that handcuffed me walked back to talk to us. He opened up the back door and said, "Can you tell me why you got a burnt shoe in the car?"

"I'm not speaking to anyone but my lawyer." I said boldly.

"As you wish." The cop said and then he slammed the door shut.

I watched him as he walked over to his partner and said a few words to him. They both looked back at me and smiled, like I was some big fucking joke. But I will have the last laugh.

"Oh my God! They are towing my freaking car!" Karin cried more dramatically as she watched everything unfold in front of us.

"But they don't have grounds to do that."

"It looks like they have grounds to me. Do you know how much it's gonna cost to get my car back?"

"Don't worry about it. I'll pay for it."

"You freaking right you're gonna pay for it." Karin hissed.

It seemed like every time I said something to Karin, the more enraged she'd become. I swear, if I could turn back the hands of time I would. I would've left her back in Maryland instead of bringing her here. She didn't deserve any of the bad treatment that she was getting.

It only took the tow truck driver a few minutes to hook up Karin's car and furnish the police officers with a copy of the towing receipt. He was literally here one minute and gone the next. I could see the pain in Karin's eyes while she watched her car get towed away.

"Ready to ride with us?" The police officer that arrested me ask.

"Can you tell me why you had her car towed away? She didn't do anything wrong?" I spoke up.

"You need to be worried about yourself and the murder charges that you're facing." He commented.

I swear, when that man uttered the words, I'm facing murder charges, it felt like he had taken the breath out of me. My eyes became glassy while a lump formed in my throat. I tried to readjust the sight of my eyes, but it seemed like every time I blinked, they would get glassier. And to put the nail in the coffin, all I could hear in my head was what the detective said to me right before I left the interview room. Fuck!!!

Cell-Mates

The look Karin gave me after the cop said that I was being charged with murder, was heartbreaking. Her whole demeanor changed that instant after the cop said what he said. She acted like she cared less about her car being towed and anything else for that matter. "I am so sorry for talking to you like I did." She whispered.

"It's okay. You had a right to say what you said. I deserved every word you said." I whispered back.

"Do you think they're really gonna charge you with murder?"

"I think they're pulling my leg to see if I'll give in. So, I'm gonna need you to keep quiet. Don't tell them anything because after I get on the phone with my lawyer, he's gonna fix everything for us."

"I hope so." Karin said and then she turned her attention back to everything going on outside the window.

The police officers took Karin and I back to the precinct where Detective Grantham was. After they pulled into the tunnel underneath the precinct, they helped us out of the car and into the intake area of the station. There was a black, female police officer on standby right after we walked through the metal detector. "I'm gonna need both of you ladies to turn around and face the wall. Put your hands on the wall so I can see them. Lay them flat." She instructed us.

"Do you have any weapons, drugs or paraphernalia on you?" She asked Karin while she began to pat down every inch of her body.

Once she was done with Karin, she walked over to where I was standing and asked me the same questions. I gave her the answer no while she searched me. "I want both of you ladies to follow me." She said as she walked alongside of us. But when we came up to a glass incased room, she instructed Karin to go into that room and then she closed the door. It locked by itself after the officer pushed it to close.

"And I want you to go in this room." She said and opened the door to a glass incase room just like the one Karin was in. After I walked into the room I turned around and said, "When will I be able to use the phone? I need to call my lawyer."

"As soon as I get word from the detective, I'll let you know." She said and then she closed the door shut.

"Fucking bitch!" I mumbled to myself.

Since Karin was in the room next to me I walked over to the wall and started banging on it. "Karin, can you hear me?" I yelled.

"Yeah, I can hear you." She yelled back.

"Are you okay?" I wanted to know.

"Yes, I'm okay. But are you okay?" She threw the question back at me.

"I will be as soon as they let me call my damn lawyer."

"Don't worry, they will."

"Are you gonna mom?"

"I don't want to because I know she's going to be upset. But I don't have anyone else to call."

"Stop yelling through the walls!" The black, female officer yelled as she banged on the glass door.

"So, I can't talk to my sister?" I yelled at the officer as she stood on the other side of the glass window.

"No, you can't." She replied. The bitch even rolled her eyes at me.

I wanted to ask her did she have a problem with me, but I didn't want to waste any energy so I said, "Well, has the detective given you authority to let me use the phone now?"

"No, he hasn't.

"Well then, why are you standing there?" I replied sarcastically while I gritted my teeth at her. I mean, was this bitch serious? She comes and tells me that I can't talk to my fucking sister through this wall or call my lawyer. But she can stand there and talk to me? I don't want to talk to her ass! I want to talk to someone that can help me get out of here.

"I'm standing here because I can. And if you don't like it then stay out of jail."

"I didn't ask to come here." I roared. This bitching was getting underneath my skin now.

"Tell that to the judge." She mocked me and then she walked off.

Pissed off with that fake ass cop, I sat down on the metal bench next to the toilet stool. The sight of this shit hole sent me into a deep depression. I mean, I didn't belong here. I hadn't done anything wrong. I just pray that when my lawyer gets here, he'll be able to work this thing out and I'll get out of here.

While I sat in this holding cell, the female officer bought in another lady and locked her in the same room with me. She was an older, white woman, that looked like a drug addict. Her hair was in disarray and her clothes looked too big for her. And when she opened her mouth to say hello, I couldn't believe that she only had a few teeth left in her mouth. This chick looked just like the walking dead. "What are you in here for?" She asked me.

"I don't know. The dumb ass cops that brought me here hasn't told me yet." I lied to her. And it was for good reason. I see stuff like this all the time on television. Cops arrest you, they put you in jail and then they find a mole to put in the same jail cell with you in hopes that you'll start talking to them and tell them all your business. Or admit to doing the crime that you were arrested for. But they won't get me caught up in that trap. No way! "So, what are you in here for?" I asked her.

"Drug possession and assault." She said. I noticed that she talked slow. It's my guess that she was still high off her drug of choice.

"Who did you assault?"

"My boyfriend. See, I was minding my own business, getting high and then he comes in the house asking me where was his money. So, I told him I didn't have his money. And then he asks me how did I get my drugs? I told him none of his business so he tries to snatch my drugs from me and that's when I stabbed him with a butter knife."

"Really? A butter knife."

"It wasn't sharp. So, he's gonna live."

While listening to this insane, ass, white lady tell me why she stabbed her boyfriend, I caught a glance of my sister Karin walking next to the black female officer as they walked by the glass. I stood up on my feet and ran to the glass window. "Karin, are you going to use the phone?" I yelled.

"I think so." She replied.

"Well, tell mom to call my lawyer." I managed to say before Karin disappeared about the corner.

"Who is that?" The white lady asked.

"It's my sister." I told her while I was making my way back to the metal bench.

"They arrested her too?" the woman wanted to know.

"Yeah, but hopefully as soon as she talks to our mother, she'll be able to leave."

"Don't bet on it. The cops in this police department are crooked as two left shoes. You'll be better off staying out of their way." The lady continued. She talked my head off for what seemed like an hour, or maybe more. I couldn't really tell because there wasn't a clock in sight. Thankfully a male police officer came from out of nowhere so I walked back up to the door and got his attention. "Sir, can you tell me what time it is?" I yelled through the glass.

He looked down at his watch and said, "It's 5:30."

"Five-thirty?" I asked him.

"Yes," he said and then started walking away.

"Is anyone gonna let me out so I can call my lawyer?" I yelled once again. But he didn't respond. He continued walking until he got out of sight.

This angered me. "Why the fuck won't they let me out of here so I can use the phone and call my lawyer?" I roared. I could feel my blood pressure rising.

"They do stuff on their own time around here. And the reason why I know is because I've been in this place so many time I've lost count."

Instead of commenting on this crazy ass lady's remark, I took a seat on the bench and buried my face in the palm of my hands.

Loose Lips Sink Ships

After sitting in that freaking holding cell for what felt like eternity, the black, female police officer opened the door and instructed me to come with her. "So, y'all are finally letting me get on the phone to talk to my lawyer?" I complained.

"Just shut your big mouth and come with me." She replied cynically.

"You do realize that I'm an adult too? Talking to me like I'm your child isn't cool." I shot back at her. I had to remind her that she needed to respect me just like she wants respect.

"Lady, just come on." She instructed me while she gave me the evil eye.

Instead of cursing this bitch out, I kept it classy and kept my mouth closed. As of this very moment, she had an advantage over me so, I figured that the less I talk, the quicker I can make shit happen. Like finally getting a chance to get on the phone to call my lawyer. Once I achieve that mission, I'm home free.

"Turn left at this corner please." She told me as she pointed at the corner coming up, connected to the next hallway.

As soon as I made that turn, my eyes lit up like a Christmas tree when I saw my sister Karin standing right in the center of this hallway. I smiled from ear to ear. She smiled back at me, so I knew she was fine. But then my smile quickly diminished after Detective Grantham joined Karin in the hallway. Immediately after he saw me, he placed his hand on her right shoulder and started thanking her for her cooperation. "I really appreciate everything you've done to move this investigation forward." I heard him say. "And because of that, I'm gonna have one of my officers take you down to the impound so you can get your vehicle. You won't have to pay either." He continued.

"Karin, what did you tell him?" I yelled at her while walking in their direction.

"It's okay, Trice. He knows everything from the guy Kevin killing Charlene and the fact that you didn't set your own house on fire. Mama, called him hours ago and told him what I told her. So, now he can go out there and arrest those guys and you don't have to worry about them doing anything to you or us." Karin explained. She gave me a look like she had just saved me from the world. But what she did was signed my death certificate.

"Do you know what you just did?" I screamed at her.

"Why are you mad?" She yelled back.

"Because you and mama just signed my death certificate!" I screamed once again and then I fell down on both of my knees and buried my face into the floor.

"Get her out of here." I heard Detective Grantham instruct someone and then I started sobbing my eyes out.

Apparently, my breakdown didn't faze any of the police officers in the station because not much longer after I had fallen down on my knees, I was lifted up by two uniform officers and dragged down the hall and taken into the room Detective Grantham was in. After I was placed in a chair near a wall, the two officers exited the room while Detective Grantham took a seat in front of me. "I told you I was gonna find out what role you played in this whole murder, arson thing, didn't I?" He bragged. But I didn't respond.

"When you finally get to speak with your mother, thank her again for me. I mean, if she hadn't called me and told me everything, you'd probably still be on the streets right now." He chuckled.

"You find this shit funny, huh?" I spat.

"No, actually I don't. An innocent woman was strangled to death and then she was tossed in an accelerant absorbed room and lit on fire because of you and those thugs." He said.

"Don't blame that shit on me! I didn't bring her to my house! When I came back from Maryland to pack up my things so I could sell my home and relocate, that whore was already inside. Her and those other niggas."

"Why were they there?"

"She lied to them and told them that I had $10,000 that belonged to her husband Leon. So, they broke into my house and waited for me to come home so they could collect."

"What happened after you entered the house?"

"I didn't do anything. I just told them that she lied to them and that's when they got mad."

"What do you mean, they got mad?"

"They got really upset because she wasted their time and they made her pay for it."

"Who killed her?"

"I don't know."

"What do you mean you don't know?"

"I don't know. They told me I could leave the house but that I had to take her son with me."

"Do you remember the names of the guys that were there?"

"Look, I've already told you enough."

"Are you protecting those guys?"

"Fuck no! I'm just not gonna get into all of that with you?"

"Your sister told me that the guy named Kevin drove up to your house in a black sedan with tinted window and threatened to kill you and your family if you snitched on him. Is that true? Because I've got patrol cars on the streets right now looking for that vehicle."

"I don't remember how the car looked." I lied. By this time, I felt like I had said enough.

"If I showed you some photos, do you think you might be able to point the suspects out?"

"Look, I'm done. I've said enough. I'm sure you got informants. Call them. They'll be able to help you."

"I'm not the one that needs help. You're the one sitting in the hot seat."

"Yeah, but you also know that I didn't do anything wrong. I didn't kill that girl and I didn't set my house on fire either."

"I don't know that for certain. But I do know that an innocent woman died in your house. Not to mention, that there is a documented history that you two hated each other."

"So, what?! Wouldn't you hate a person if they consistently tried create havoc in your life?"

"I'm not sure what I would do." He replied nonchalantly. But I knew he was being a smart-ass.

"So, what's gonna happen now?" I wanted to know. I had been in this fucking place long enough.

"If you don't help me find the real killers then I'm gonna have to put the charges on you."

It felt like a stack of bricks hit me in the chest. I was being charged with murder? Was this fucking cop serious? I didn't kill that bitch! Those niggas did, so why do I have to suffer the consequences? This is wrong.

On the verge of tears, I looked at the detective and said, "I wanna call my lawyer."

He stood up on his feet and then he started reading my Miranda rights. When he was done, he instructed one of the police officers to escort me out of the room. "Take her out of here and book her on murder and arson charges."

"Wait, so y'all aren't gonna let me call my lawyer?!" I screamed as tears started tumbling down my face.

"Let her call her lawyer too." Detective Grantham said and then he exited the room.

Another Devastating Blow

I can't believe that I was charged with Charlene's murder. What was the world coming to? Looking back on my life, I never thought that I would allow myself to be in this type of situation. Murder? Arson? Really? I swear, I need to wake up from this nightmare.

After I was finger printed and processed, I had to see a magistrate to see what my bail was going to be. Unfortunately for me, the fucking red-neck didn't give me shit. "No bail." He said. Boy, did that devastated me. As far as I know, I'm gonna be in this place until I can prove my innocence in court. But I don't think that I can be in here that long. I've seen cases on TV where people would commit suicide. I might just consider that as an option.

I was transported to the county jail not far from the police station. One of the correctional officers put me in a cellblock with eight other women. Some looked like drug addicts, prostitutes, you name it, and that's what they looked like.

"Need some help with making your bed?" A young, black woman asked me. She was about my size, so I figured that if something jumped off, then I would be able to take her down with no problems.

"No, I got it. But thanks." I told her.

"Well, my name is Pam. And if you need anything, just let me know.

"Okay, I will." I said. But in reality, I wasn't going to ask her for shit. We're in the same fucking jail so what could she possibly do for me? "Oh wait, where is the phone?" I asked her while she was walking away.

"It's over there on the wall." She pointed out. "You get a free 5-minute phone call and then after that, your family is going to have to start up a phone account." She continued.

"Thank you." I said. Getting a free 5-minute phone call made me feel like I had just won the lottery so I headed in that direction. I couldn't wait to get on the phone. I called my attorney while I was at the police station but I wasn't able to get in contact with him. So, this call will be strictly for my mother. She is the only person that could get me out of this shit storm I was in. I mean, if she hadn't called the cop and opened her fucking mouth then, I wouldn't be here. So, she owes me big time.

I called her cellphone and thankfully it started ringing. On the third ring my call was answered. "Hello, mom." I said. I was so anxious to talk to her because I had a laundry list of shit I needed for her to do.

"Nah, this ain't your mama." I heard a male's voice say.

"What? Wait, who is this?" I asked him. I was confused. I mean, did I dial the wrong number.

"Bitch, you know who it is. Remember I told you that I was gonna kill you and your family if you didn't keep your word shut."

"I did."

"No, you didn't. And now I'm about to show you who I really am."

Before I could utter another word, the call went radio silent. "Hello," I yelled. "Hello!" I yelled again. And then I started hitting the base of the phone with the receiver. "He's gonna kill my family!" I screamed while I continued to bang the receiver against the base of it.

"Somebody stop her!" I heard one of the inmates say in the back ground.

"Why don't you do it?" I heard another inmate say.

But it didn't matter what anyone of them said, my family is about to be murdered and I couldn't do anything to help them.

"Fuck!" I screamed one last time and then I collapsed onto the floor.

Sneak Peek into-

ERICKA KANE

Prologue

My naked body shivered as my blood ran down my face, chest, and stomach. I couldn't stop my legs from shaking. Not to mention, my bladder felt like it would explode at any moment. Wherever they had me, it was literally freezing cold like I was naked in Alaska.

"Hit her again," a man's voice boomed. I braced myself because I knew exactly what was coming next. "Please," I whispered, but my words were ignored. It was clear that these were some very dangerous people and they were not going to have any mercy on me. It also became clear that if I ever got out of here alive, I would go on a serious mission to hunt down each and every one of these motherfuckers and torture them ten times worse than they did to me.

"Agggh!" I let out another scream as I felt the shock waves from the oversized stun gun that was being used to torture me. It had to be something they use on large farm animals to make them submissive. I didn't know how many more high-powered surges of electricity my body would be able to take.

My face was scrunched up and my eyes rolled into the back of my head. Sweat was pouring from every pore on my body. I gagged but nothing came up from my stomach. I was in so much pain I felt like even the organs inside of my body hurt. My heart pounded painfully against my weakened chest bone and my stomach literally churned. I was wishing for death because even that had to be better than what I was feeling at the moment. Another hit with the electric current caused piss to spill from my bladder and splash on the feet of one of my tormentors.

"This bitch pissed on me!" he growled. Then he took his huge hand and slapped me across the face so hard spit shot out of my mouth.

"Daddy! Help me!" I struggled to get the words out as my body jerked fiercely from another hit from the stun gun.

"Please let her go," my father mumbled, his words coming out labored and almost breathless. "Just take me, but let her go," he whispered through his battered lips. I had heard him coughing and wheezing as our captors beat him unmercifully. It was almost unreal what we were going through. As hard as the torture was, it was even harder to see my father in a position of total helplessness. He had always been my hero all of my life. When my mother decided that she didn't want to be a mother anymore, it had been my father who'd made all of the sacrifices to take care of me alone. He was always so strong and heroic to me, but now, he was just as weak and useless as me.

"Daddy," I panted, my head hanging. "Don't let them kill me."

I squinted through my battered eyes and tried to see him, but the bright lights my torturers were using prevented me from catching a real good glimpse of my father. I figured that I would probably never see him again. I could hear the voices around me clearly though, so I knew we were all in close proximity.

"You betrayed us, Eric. You and your little bitch daughter thought you could outsmart us. I should have never trusted you as a business partner. I should have known that such a weak man, who would run from his native country, would give in to these American ideals. You were once a son of Nigeria…a man who loved his country, now a traitor, a betrayer, and a weak ass man. You got too big for yourself. I knew when you came to this country you would think you were the boss of everything. I let you have a good life here. Yes, you were living in a big mansion, rubbing elbows with the wealthy white Americans that you wished you could call your brothers, and most of all working with the police to bite the hand that feeds you," a tall, ugly man with black skin and yellow eyes hissed as he came into focus in my vision. He had stepped around the bright light and I could see every feature of his hideous face. He resembled a Gorilla because there was something grotesque about his features. His nostrils were almost non-existent and those little beady eyes didn't look like they belonged on a human face at all.

"No. I did everything you asked, Kesso. I was always loyal to you and my entire country and my fellow Nigerians. I helped all of the people you sent to me. I gave them jobs. I gave them money. I gave them places to stay. I repaid my debts to you over and over again. I entered into this business unwillingly, but I did it to repay the debts I owed you for helping me get to America. I turned over everything you asked for…including all of the slaves you wanted. All of the money you wanted, even my wife. You even took the only woman that I ever truly loved from me. What more could I do, Kesso? Now, you have my daughter," my father cried as another round of punches landed in his midsection. More cracks and coughs came as the men pounded on my father, breaking bones and injuring his insides. I heard my father's words, but I couldn't believe my ears. Did my mother run to my father's business partner? Did my father get into something that he would never be able to get out of? It was a lot to handle because I had always worshipped the ground that my father walked upon. My heart was breaking watching him suffer. It was worse than any pain my torturers could impose on me right then.

"Daddy! Stop hurting my Daddy!" It was killing me to know he was in all of that pain. After I discovered what my father was into I was devastated, but that didn't change the fact that I loved him and that he was all that I had in the world. I recognized that the position we were in right at that moment was my fault too. My father had pleaded with me to leave the situation alone. He had asked me to stop investigating and to stop trying to dig up the truth. My father had actually pleaded with me to just accept everything the way it was, but I couldn't do it. He knew how stubborn I could be, but there was nothing much he could do about it. I had to keep investigating for myself. I had to call in the assistance of the police. I wanted justice! That was the stubbornness in me that I had gotten from my mother. She was the type of bitch that never backed down from something that she wanted. As much as I hated her, I was like her in a lot of ways...all of her bad ways. Now, my father and I were facing death with no clear way out of the situation. All because of me! If anyone deserved to die, it was me.

"Daddy I'm so sorry! I just wanted to help. I just wanted to make things better. I just needed some answers. I never meant to have this happen to you. I told you Kesso! Just kill me and let my father go! It is me that you want! I was the one who brought all of the heat to your door and pulled the lid off of your business! It was all me...not my father!" I cried some more. I bet this so-called African prince wasn't used to a woman speaking to him like that. I hated him and I didn't care about any traditions.

"Shut her up! I'm tired of her fucking mouth. This little bitch cost me millions of dollars because she wanted to play Nancy Drew...now I want to see her suffer. She's a piece of shit just like her father. She is not worth sharing the same air with," Kesso, the ugly man barked, waving his hands. His goons immediately surrounded me. My heart rattled in my chest, but there was nothing else they could do to me that would hurt me more than the possibility of my father dying at my hands. I gave up at that moment. Whatever was going to happen must've been our fate from the beginning, I reasoned with myself. I kept screaming things that I knew were disrespectful in the eyes of my father's Nigerian counterparts. I wasn't going to be one of those passive women. No! I knew what those bastards were doing to women and I could only hope that the call I had made before they snatched me would help me in the end.

After a few minutes, one of those huge, wrestler type dudes grabbed me by my hair and dragged me across the gravel floor. "Agh!" I screamed. It was like nothing I had ever felt before. I don't know how I didn't slip into shock after all of those hours of torture I had endured. My entire body felt like someone had doused me with gasoline and lit me on fire. I could feel the once perfect skin on my legs and ass shedding away against the rough floor. I didn't want to die, but if I was going to die, I was going to go out fighting. I tucked my bottom lip under my top teeth and gritted.

"Get off of me! Get the fuck off of me!" I screeched so loud that my throat itched. "Fuck all of you! You're all going to burn in hell for what you're doing!" I continued; feeling blood rushing to places on my body that I didn't know even existed. I bucked my body wildly, but all of my fighting efforts were to no avail. Of course they were stronger than me, which meant that I wasn't going to be able to break free. I never dreamed of going out of this life fighting tooth and nail. My father always called me his little African lion and I planned to live up to that name before I died. The man dragging me finally let go of the fist full of my hair he had been holding. He released me with so much force that my head slammed to the floor. I felt something at the base of my skull come loose. I was dazed for a few seconds, but not for long. I was brought back to reality when I felt a boot slam into my ribs. The force was so great that a mouthful of blood spurted from my mouth.

"You don't have such a big mouth now, huh?" the goon hissed, his accent thick and barely understandable.

"Please don't hurt her anymore. I will give you everything I have if you just let her go," I heard my father gurgle.

"It is too late for that. You and your little troublemaker should've thought about that before both of you betrayed me. Now, someone has to pay with their life. There will be no more talking," Kesso said with finality. The next thing I heard was the ear-shattering explosion of a gun.

"No!!!!!" I belted out, right before my entire world fell apart. Blackness engulfed me and I wondered how it had all come to this. Not even a month ago, my father and I had been so happy.

ERICKA KANE

Chapter 1 *Celebration*

<u>ONE MONTH EARLIER</u>

"**H**appy Birthday to you…happy birthday to you…happy birthday dear Ericka…" the entire room sang to me in unison. The song was one that I had associated with big expensive gifts and lots of visitors all of my life. My father never let my birthday go by without something big, whether it was a party, loads of gifts or a trip to some far away exotic place. This year he had succeeded in surprising me with the biggest party I'd had since my sweet sixteen and I was elated. It was the best party I had ever had and trust me when I say, I had had some big fiestas.

I smiled so hard my cheeks ached. It was my day and everyone knew it. Even the paparazzi, who was totally obsessed with my family, was allowed to come in and snap a few pictures. That surprised me too, because my father always hated the fact that those aggressive photographers always seemed to catch us at our worst. Flashing lights and those picture thirsty photographers screaming for me to look at their cameras made this event feel like a real celebrity party. Not to mention a few famous faces sprinkled in the crowd. My father had more than one celebrity client and they had come out just for me.

As everyone came to the end of the Happy Birthday song, my father held up his hand and flashed his perfect porcelain veneered smile. He was truly a distinguished gentleman, standing a handsome six foot, three inches tall with a very lean build. Even for his age, my father didn't have those old man guts. He stayed in the gym five days a week and he played tennis on the weekends. He took great care of himself and it didn't go unnoticed. My father wore a very neat salt and pepper speckled goatee, which made his pecan colored skin look rich and smooth. His tailor-made Armani suit and his diamond cuff links screamed wealth. Although he was a second generation Nigerian, my father was mixed with white so his skin wasn't as dark as his other family members. I saw quite a few older and younger women in the crowd swooning over him. My father opened is mouth to speak and captivated the entire room. The crowd that had surrounded my custom made five-tier, Swarovski crystal adorned birthday cake lowered their voices to listen to his baritone. My father could command attention anywhere he went. I always thought he should've gone into politics, but I guess being a native of Nigeria would prevent him from doing that here in the United States. I looked on proudly. Even at his age, my father was hot!

"Good evening everyone. May I have your full attention on this beautiful occasion that we share," my father, the distinguished Nigerian diplomat, Eric Mumbutu, also known in America as Eric Kane, yelled out, quieting the huge crowd. I felt all tingly inside just listening to him. His accent was still noticeable, but not enough to make him seem like he couldn't speak English.

"I brought you all here tonight to help me celebrate my beautiful daughter, Ericka's birthday. It is a bittersweet moment for me, because I can remember the day she was born like it was yesterday. I have sacrificed everything to make sure that my little girl always had the best of everything. I know what it is like to have hardships, so I never wanted my Ericka, my namesake, to suffer any hardships. As of today, she is no longer a baby. She has blossomed into a wonderful woman that has bestowed a great sense of pride to our family name. I am so proud of her and all of the things she has accomplished. At this ripe age of twenty-five she has brought me nothing but joy. To you my daughter, I love you more than life itself and as your father, I will always be here for you," my father beamed, raising his champagne glass high above his head. "Cheers!" Everyone followed his lead. I was on the brink of tears. My father had completely raised me alone after my mother decided that she wanted her own life in Los Angeles. I had never bonded with her, but I had an unbreakable bond with my father. She hadn't even bothered to show up to the party...some social event that she just couldn't get out of was the excuse she used to ditch my party. She had never been a mother to me anyway so I didn't expect much from her.

"Aww daddy! I love you too and I am proud that you are my daddy. Even at twenty-five I will always be your baby girl. I strive to make you proud and keep our family name pure like you always asked," I replied throwing my arms around his neck. My father picked me up off my feet and bear hugged me. The crowd cheered and the sound of glasses clinking filled the air like music. It was one of the happiest moments of my life. My father placed me back on the floor and I couldn't stop smiling. The music picked back up and the crowd began buzzing again.

"Now go enjoy the night. We are paying this DJ and this band to bring you the party of a lifetime," my father joked, planting a kiss on my cheek.

When I turned around the first thing I saw was the beautiful, caramel, smiling face of my best friend, Tia. I rushed over to her, my chest swollen with happiness. She was happy for me I could tell, because she was showing all of her perfectly straight, gleaming white teeth.

"Eww girl, I just love how close you are with your father. And this party right here is just absolutely gorgeous. You will be the talk of the DMV after this. I'm sure it will hit TMZ and all of the other blogs. Your daddy showed you love with this shindig," Tia chimed.

"He really out did himself this time, right? He never ceases to amaze me...that man loves me from here to the moon. I thought it got no better than my sweet sixteen because I had Lil Wayne perform and all of those ice sculptures that night...remember? But this...this is amazing," I said as I looked out on the place my father had chosen—a top notch catering hall that overlooked the Potomac River. The room was decorated all pink and green in honor of my sorority colors. My father had spared no expense. Three-foot tall floral centerpieces with pink and green roses, lilies and hydrangeas sat at the center of all of the tables. The gold chair covers and the beautiful green and pink place settings gave the room a classy air. The five piece live band played original songs my father had composed just for me and he also had DJ Switch, a high profile celebrity DJ spinning music when the band took a break. Each of my guests was going home with a gold bottle of Ace of Spades that had my name engraved on the outside. That alone had to have cost my father hundreds of thousands of dollars. My father had definitely gone all out for my twenty-fifth birthday celebration. I couldn't be more grateful.

Seriously, he had me so spoiled I didn't know if any man could ever live up to my expectations.

"I don't know what the wedding is going to look like after this," Tia replied, opening her arms wide. "I still can't get over the hot ass DJ. Do you realize that he plays music for celebrities and he is on the radio for gawd sakes," she quipped. I laughed. Of course I knew who DJ Switch was!

"You know I'm spoiled as hell, Tia. But don't front your father is going to hook you up too next month when you turn the big two five too," I reminded her. Tia blushed because she knew it was true. We were both spoiled rotten from the time we were little girls. We had nothing but the best growing up—private schools, dance, gymnastics, acting classes, equestrian classes, tennis lessons and crew lessons. Sorry to say, none of those things mattered of course because Tia and I just loved shopping, partying and being little social butterflies. We were definitely on equal footing when it came to having things.

"If your father flew that hot ass dress in all the way from Paris for you to wear to my party, you know he is going all out when it's your turn to have a party. He'll probably buy you an even more expensive dress to cover this ass," I joked, slapping her on her thick, round ass playfully. Tia burst into laughter. That's what we did all of the time. We joked, we argued, we shopped, we hung out and we were inseparable most of the time. I couldn't remember one single day not speaking to Tia since we had become friends. Even when we were forced to go on our family vacations overseas each of us would find a way to call one another. I called Tia my Siamese twin. We had each other's backs.

"You're probably right, but still this party is no laughing matter. I had a fucking blast tonight. Honestly, I haven't even been to a club and had as good a time lately" Tia complimented. I hugged her and laughed. The champagne was taking a hold of my senses and Tia's too. She always got real mushy when she was tipsy.

"I love you BFF," Tia said.

"Ditto, chick," I said back.

Tia had been my best friend since we were eleven years old. Both of us came from wealthy families. I met Tia when she moved from France to Northern Virginia. It was an instant friendship. We were two of the very few rich black girls that went to our school; all of the other girls were snobby white girls.

"Come with me to the bathroom. I got something for you. It's the best birthday gift you'll receive all night. Trust me, it's like nothing you've ever had before. You won't regret it at all," Tia yelled in my ear over the loud music. I already knew what it was. That was the one thing that was different about us; Tia had always been way more daring and willing to try new things than I was. She experimented with new drugs almost daily. I wasn't really the type that liked getting high, especially not as much as Tia did. Tia could see the apprehension in my facial expression.

"It's your fucking birthday, don't get scary tonight. Live a little. I shouldn't have to bend your arm to make you feel good. You know you want to get that feeling that we've been chasing since the very first time...c'mon stop acting like you don't," Tia chastised as she grabbed my arm and pulled me towards the clear, mirrored spiral steps that led from the main ballroom to the private bathroom and dressing room suite for the guest of honor.

Tia used her shoulder to push open the doors and she yanked me through the large, gold doors and locked it behind us. Her eyes were wide and she was breathing hard, like what ever she had to show or tell me was really urgent. I never got that excited over drugs. For a quick moment, I wondered if that meant Tia was addicted.

"Ericka, you have to promise to be down with me this time," Tia said almost breathlessly. Sweat was lining up at her hairline making her brassy, blonde hair curl up near her forehead. I crinkled my face. I was always down with my best friend, I just wasn't sure that being down meant trying something that might get me addicted. Getting on drugs was a sure way to make my father die of a broken heart.

"This is some new shit you have never tried. Trust me, premium is an understatement. I got it from my mother's dealer, Cinco. He is sweet on me too so he hooked me up with an extra fat bundle. I'm thinking that he wants to fuck me, but I'm not sure," Tia bragged, putting her exclusive, lavender colored Chanel caviar bag up on the granite counter top. I twisted my lips at what she was saying. Tia was getting into this shit too heavy for me. It had gone beyond experimenting with weed like we had done at thirteen, or sniffing a line or two of coke at a party like we had done at seventeen.

"I didn't like it the last time. I don't know if I'm down with this. You know I'll do anything for you T…but I think you're getting a little too deep with this now. It seems like you are doing this every time we are together," I said apprehensively. Tia rolled her eyes and sighed. I looked at her real good in the light. She was still strikingly beautiful, but she looked like a fiend salivating over drugs right then. I squinted my eyes as she dumped a small mountain of the drug onto the back of her hand. Tia stood almost six feet tall with long, slender legs, a tiny waist, and a flat stomach with large cosmetically placed boobs. Tia's slanted grey cat eyes against her caramel skin and naturally thick, Beyoncé blonde hair made her look like an exotic beauty that should be gracing the cover of Sport Illustrated or some high fashion magazine. She had inherited the best features of her Brazilian father and her African-American mother. I mean, I wasn't a slouch in the looks department either. My skin was lighter than Tia's, almost the color of butter. I guess my father being African couldn't hold up to my mother being white. I had the deepest, darkest, brown eyes and my thick black eyelashes always caught people's attention. My thick, long, hair was naturally jet-black. My personal hairstylist always told me that people would die to have their natural hair color as rich as mine. I was shorter than Tia, but I had a small waist, round hips and an ass to match hers. I hadn't gone under the knife for new boobs yet, but Tia had because her father was a plastic surgeon. That night I wore a banging Nicole Miller mini dress with the entire back out. It wasn't as exclusive as Tia's dress that had been flown in from Paris, but it served me just fine. I was never jealous of my beautiful friend, but I also knew I wasn't as exotic looking and pretty as Tia was. I kept watching her and thinking that if she continued using drugs she wasn't going to be so beautiful for long.

"Stop being scary, Ericka. It is still experimenting. I am not addicted if that's what you're trying to imply," Tia retorted. "Now don't be a baby all of your life. Remember you just turned twenty-five yesterday."

"What does my birthday have to do with it?"

"It has everything to do with it. Now watch me work."

Tia placed her nose on top of the mound of happy dust on her hand and inhaled like a high-powered vacuum cleaner. When she finished there was absolutely nothing left on her hand so I was amazed. I didn't even see any residue. Tia was a fucking pro at sniffing lines, obviously.

"Uh!" she grunted as her legs went weak. I thought she would fall, but she just stumbled around all the while keeping her balance. "Whoa! Hot damn!" She shouted and then she started laughing although neither of us had told a joke. Tia was doing some crazy dance. She kicked off her Louboutin heels and jumped around like a white girl trying to dance. It was crazy to watch. After a few seconds, I guess she remembered that it was my turn. Tia went back over to her bag, got the good out and began getting some of the drugs ready for me.

"Ericka...do it! It's my birthday gift to you. C'mon...it'll make you forget all about that dickhead Cyrus," Tia slurred, still laughing without anything being funny.

When she brought up my ex-boyfriend Cyrus, the hairs on my skin stood up. I felt my heart swell with pain and that was all I needed as a battery in my back. Tia always knew how to tug at my heartstrings and get me to bend to her will. Tia had a small pile of the drugs ready for me.

"Don't be scared birthday girl. Just take it in and forget all of your troubles. It works wonders," Tia whispered like she was my fairy godmother speaking in my ear. I knew better. I didn't have a good gut feeling about it, but I couldn't say no. I swept my long hair aside and bent down, but before I inhaled, I asked, "What is this shit? It's not white; it's like a bluish color. I've never seen anything like this before." The concern was definitely underlying my words. Not that I was going to back down from my strong willed friend, but I had to ask. It was the only stand I would make.

"Yes boo! It is a new blue crystal meth called arctic ice. We are the first people to get our hands on it. I guess that is the perks of being rich bitches. I'm telling you E...you will never be the same after you try this shit. It is not made in some dirty meth lab. This was made in like a full state of the art scientific lab. Only us rich folks can afford even an ounce of this shit right here. Cinco said we could use half the amount and get doubly as high as regular crystal. It's preemo, nothing like that fucking homemade Drano type of shit," Tia explained, giggling the whole time like she was giddy as hell. One thing I must say, the drug was lasting a long time in her system so I knew it was pretty potent. Knowing that made my apprehension about trying it even stronger.

I had always had a hard time telling my best friend no. So, with hundreds of party guests right above celebrating me, I was locked in a bathroom against my better judgment experimenting with God knows what kind of new drug she had gotten her manicured fingers on.

"Let's go Ericka. You're not going to leave me to experience all of this happiness alone are you? Stop being a baby. Get your mind off of Cyrus. Show yourself a good time. Don't walk around with a stick up your ass all of your life. Don't be a daddy's girl forever. Life is for living," Tia kept on prodding and prodding.

"Ok! Ok! Just shut the fuck up! You sound like a damn broken record," I snapped. And finally I relented. Most of the time I just did whatever Tia wanted to do because she was one of those strong personalities that would hound you until you just gave up.

I flared my nostrils and breathed in as hard as I could. Probably not as deep as Tia had sniffed, but deep enough for the little blue particles to fly up my nose. I swear it was like someone had slammed a hammer into my forehead. That blast was powerful as hell.

"Ah!" I stumbled backwards. I immediately threw my hand up over my nose as tears involuntarily danced down my eyes. As the drugs took its place in the membranes of my nose it started to feel like someone had shoved two fire lit sticks up each of my nostrils. The pain radiated all the way up to my brain. Tia was laughing hysterically at my reaction. I was bouncing on my legs and flailing my arms. It was all I could do to keep from screaming in agony.

"Oh shit. What the fuck Tia?" I cringed as I shook my head trying to get the pain to stop. Within seconds my entire body felt different—lighter. The pain subsided seemingly as quickly as it had started. My muscles began relaxing too. Suddenly I was feeling euphoric; I guess this was the extreme high Tia was referring to because the entire room began looking like a rainbow of colors dancing on the walls. I swayed on my legs and my eyeballs moved rapidly without me telling them to.

"You're feeling it aren't you? Ha! I told you this was like nothing we had ever tried before. Fuck that purple kush shit we started off with because this shit here is the new aged stuff. That outer space experience," Tia cheered, elated that I was down with her now. I was feeling light on my feet as the drugs continued to ease my senses. I stumbled around trying to find a chair because I felt like my knees were melting like butter against the sun. I couldn't front there was something superb about the way I was feeling. My skin was even sensitive to the touch. Tia was right. Whatever was in the new blue stuff was unlike anything we had ever tried out before. I didn't want to admit that I wanted another hit, but I think secretly someplace deep down inside, I really did want to suck in another nose full of that shit.

Finally, I slumped down into one of the vanity chairs. Small swirls of colorful lights began clouding my vision. My lips began curling into a smile, but I wasn't telling them to smile. I was kind of aware now that I had no control over my own body parts. I felt like singing and dancing and jumping around. I couldn't move even if I wanted to. I hung onto the chair for dear life because every few seconds I could feel myself slipping off the side. I truly felt like my body was made of jelly.

Tia's mouth was moving but I couldn't hear her. My ears were filled with noise that I had no clue where it was coming from. It sounded like little angels playing instruments around me. I waved my hand at Tia as I watched her dump another small mound onto her hand and in my head I was saying don't do it, but my mouth wouldn't move. I didn't think she needed to take anymore. A quick thought came into my head of my father finding out about our little experiment and a flash of panic flitted through my stomach. I tried to wave at Tia again, but again, my hand wouldn't cooperate with the signals from my brain.

Tia turned towards me and did a little happy dance. Dancing for drugs? Right then and there I knew she had to be addicted. Only drug addicts danced for drugs and got that happy over getting high.

"Ain't no nigga like the one I got...right here this blue ice fucks me better," Tia sang mocking the Foxxy Brown song. I couldn't even laugh at her silly ass. But, I watched as Tia deeply inhaled the second little mountain of the blue stuff in through her nose. Her reaction was instantaneous. "Oww!" Tia belted out. She bent over at the waist for a few seconds. That's how powerful that shit was—it even made her ass weak in the knees. Then Tia stumbled over to me, took a small amount of the arctic ice meth and placed it up against my left nostril. I didn't want to inhale it, but as soon as I took a breath the drugs disappeared up my nasal cavity. It hit my brain within seconds and more tears danced down the sides of my eyes. This time it didn't hurt as bad but the buzz took me through a vortex of time and reality. Shit started spinning in the room and I felt like I could just fly. My eyes were moving even more rapidly than before. My heart was pounding like I had run miles and miles at top speed. It beat so hard that I could even feel it throbbing in my throat. Sweat poured down the sides of my face. I was sure that my professionally done makeup looked a cakey mess by now.

I watched as Tia spun around in front of me. She was moving like a true drug addict. Like she was speeding. I couldn't move, I literally felt buried alive in my own body. I was screaming and saying things in my head, but my mouth would not move. Tia danced and jumped around for what seemed like an eternity. Finally, she had worn herself down until her body finally collapsed to the floor. My mouth opened but I couldn't scream. I could hear something that sounded like heavenly harps playing in my ears and I suddenly felt like I was suspended in the air over the room. There were a lot of bright lights clouding my eyes. It was so bright I started squinting. My vision and my hearing began to fade away that instant. I could hear my heart slowing down too. The next thing I felt was some unknown force lifting me up from the chair as if I was suspended on a piece of rope. I could feel some cold breeze whipping around me. I remember shivering, but was unable to cover myself with my hands. I didn't know if I was dying or what, but suddenly I was looking down from the ceiling at my best friend and myself. How was that even possible? I was plastered to the ceiling looking at myself in the same room. I felt like throwing up, but nothing came up. I was not inside of my body, which was painfully clear now. Now I know what people meant when they said out of body experience.

From my sudden aerial view, I could see that Tia was sprawled haphazardly on the hard, marble floor of the upscale bathroom. Her beautiful, model like long legs were splayed in an awkward position that looked like it was causing her a lot of pain. Tia resembled a broken Barbie doll that some little girl had twisted into awkward positions and discarded. As for me, as I looked down at myself, I could see that I was lying flat on my back after falling out of the vanity chair. My mouth hung open, my eyes were wide staring straight up at nothing and my hair lay around me like a black death shroud.

"Get up Ericka! Get up and go get help Ericka!" I was screaming at myself but nothing happened. I was stuck on that ceiling looking down, but the Ericka that was on the floor was stiff. I couldn't move from either place. I couldn't call for help because no one could hear a dead girl. I couldn't breathe because that throbbing in my heart had already stopped. I couldn't help Tia or myself. I was powerless and I couldn't find her. I wondered if Tia was with me up on the ceiling looking down at us too. I wondered if she was screaming for help or screaming at herself to get up off that bathroom floor and help her best friend. I wondered if Tia was regretting giving me the drugs in the first place. It was useless trying to figure shit out. I was clearly in a different realm. I didn't know if I was going to be stuck there forever or if someone would eventually find us. This real was one that I couldn't understand then and probably would never be able to speak about again. Tia and I both were either too high to move from the ugly positions we lay in or too dead from an overdose to control what was happening to us. I had probably died at my twenty-fifth birthday party. If that was the case, I was sure that I had probably broken my father's heart into a million little pieces. "I'm sorry daddy. I never meant to hurt you when you were only trying to celebrate me," I said from my position on the ceiling. After that everything went bright white. I am dead. That was the last thing I remember thinking.

ERICK KANE – IN STORES NOW!!